The Secret In The Walls

A Moon Shadows Mystery

Sherry Briscoe

Chat Noir Press

www.sherrybriscoe.com

Boise, Idaho

A Moon Shadows Mystery

Book 1 – Fine Line of Denial
Book 2 – The Secret in the Walls

Be sure to sign up for notices of new books coming out at www.sherrybriscoe.com.

Sherry Briscoe
Boise, Idaho
www.sherrybriscoe.com

Publisher's Note: This is a work of fiction. Names, characters, places, and incidents are a product of the author's imagination. Locales and public names are sometimes used for atmospheric purposes. Any resemblance to actual people, living or dead, or to businesses, companies, events, institutions, or locales is completely coincidental.

Book Layout © 2017 BookDesignTemplates.com

The Secret In The Walls
ISBN 978-1-7329495-2-2

Dedicated to Darryl, my inspiration for this book.
Thank you for introducing me to your friends and the
Casino Bar in Ketchum, Idaho. What a fun and
magical place.

*"A secret's worth depends on the people from
whom it must be kept."*

—CARLOS RUIZ ZAFON

CONTENTS

CHAPTER ONE

Sliding in the flip flops he'd fished out of a dumpster, Victor Nellis stumbled into the Alibi, a small bar three blocks from the U.C. Berkley campus. The air was sultry with a tinge of stale beer and polished wood that moved on the edges of ceiling fans. He shuffled across the room with his hands shoved deep in the pockets of his cargo shorts, shoulders hunched forward and head hung down looking only at the floor beneath his feet and his ridged, yellow toenails.

Lucky for Victor it was happy hour. He had just enough change on him for one beer. He glanced past the bartender filling his glass, to the mirror behind the bar. Victor almost didn't recognize himself, his blue eyes were dulled and his face was covered in scroungy stubble, pale and splotchy with sores from years of drug use. He was thirty-two, but hard living had aged him rapidly. His shoulder-length blond hair was still wet from the shower he'd just taken in The Mission homeless shelter. He hadn't eaten a decent meal in two days, but more than food, he craved a fix. His hands shook and his breathing was erratic.

Victor shuffled toward a vacant table with two chairs near the end of the bar. Dim lights hung over a pool table and a dart board on one wall. It was easy for him to disappear in the shadows. He flinched every time the bartender clinked glasses or rang a sale on the register. Sounds sent sparks through his veins that bordered on painful. He clutched his beer and watched the crowd of college students, waiting for a chance to grab a purse or lift a wallet. Maybe even swipe a tip off a table while no one was looking.

Victor was a desperate man. He owed money he couldn't pay, craved drugs he couldn't buy, and had secrets he could never tell. Cold sweats surged through his body and his tongue felt thick in his mouth. He mumbled incoherent thoughts as he looked around the room.

Brushing his hair out of his face, Victor took a sip of beer and locked sites on a clean cut college boy who came in with two girls. They all dropped their backpacks on one chair at a table near the far end of the bar and ordered a pitcher of beer. Victor's mouth watered in anticipation as he watched them.

The girls were attractive and giggled a lot. But Victor was more interested in the guy. He'd paid for the beer with cash and stuffed the change back in his wallet. Victor ran several scenarios through his mind. He could accidentally bump into the guy's chair, spilling his beer on him and lifting the wallet in the confusion. He could follow the guy into the men's room. Or maybe just follow him home. His mind was reeling with possibilities. He let out a small chuckle at the prospect. He imagined the soothing warmth of heroin melting through his veins.

Riddled with expectation, Victor left his table and took a seat at the bar near his target. He needed to pick up some conversation he could use. He listened intently.

"Do you ever see anyone famous in your dad's bar?" asked the girl with waist long brown hair and a multi-colored sleeve tattoo of Chinese art on her left arm.

"Sure, Sun Valley's home to quite a few stars. But my dad's favorite was Ernest Hemingway. He's got pictures of him all over the place."

"He's a writer, right?"

"A dead writer," the guy replied.

"Oh, that's right. I remember something about him in English Lit. Didn't he commit suicide, like, a long time ago?" the girl asked. The other girl, the one with a short Afro sat quiet and drank her beer.

"Yep, in the early sixties. That's the one."

A group of five college-aged guys came in laughing and raving about a football game and sat a few stools down the bar from Victor. He had to strain to hear the Sun Valley boy with all the cash. He carefully watched the trio's reflections in the bar mirror. Then as luck would have it, Afro girl stood up and started for the bar when she turned back and called out, "Hey Doug, you want another pitcher?"

"Doug," Victor murmured to himself, memorizing the name. He could strike up a conversation now. Victor's fingers twitched as he rubbed his hand through his hair. He watched his mark finish his beer, stand up and say something to the girl with long hair. He noticed Doug's clothes, Hilfiger polo shirt, designer jeans, expensive, neat. The guy was from money, Victor could smell it.

Victor sucked on his bottom lip as he watched Doug make his way to the men's room in the back of the bar. His pulse pounded in his ears. He turned and glanced at the two girls and smiled. They twisted their faces at him, then broke out laughing. He clenched his jaw. Victor used to come here to pick up chicks, back when he was in school. But he had dropped out his third year when the heroin took over his life. Now school didn't matter anymore. Neither did chicks. He just needed a fix. He needed college boy Doug's money.

"Hey, I gotta' get going," Doug said as he walked back to the table. "I'll catch up with you tomorrow?" He grabbed his backpack, leaned over and gave each of the girls a hug.

Victor didn't take his gaze off of the bulging wallet in Doug's back pocket. He finished his beer in one gulp and scooted out the front door ahead of his mark.

Victor waited.

The door swung open and Doug stepped out by himself. He ran a hand through his curly brown hair and glanced at his expensive-looking watch.

"Doug, is that you?" Victor leaned against the brick wall taking a drag from a cigarette. "From like...Sun Valley?" he said as Doug passed him. Cornering his prey was intoxicating. The edge of his lip twitched with excitement. "Don't your folks own the..." He took a long drag off his cigarette and waited for Doug to fill in the blank.

"Sorry, I don't recognize..." Doug took a step back.

"Yeah man, like, I've...you were a kid, junior high, maybe. I remember you. Like, that bar is the coolest up there..with..." Victor coughed, wiped his mouth with the back of his hand and stepped out of the direct light from the bar. "Damn it, what's the name of the place?" He threw his hands up and chuckled trying to look non-threatening.

"So I've seen you in the Casino in Ketchum?" Doug asked tightening his grip on the straps of his backpack.

"Yeah dude, like, that's the place. I love that bar. So, like, what's your dad doing these days?" Victor ran a shaky hand through his hair again and pulled one side behind an ear.

"Oh, they're vacationing. They sold the bar last month, so now they're just out spending all my inheritance," Doug laughed. He kept looking at Victor as if he was trying to remember him. "Well, I gotta' get home."

"Yeah, me too. You, like, live this direction?" Victor puffed on his cigarette while keeping pace with Doug. "So, like, did that bum you out? I mean, them selling the place? Usually the kids, like, get to take the family business."

"They wanted the money now and I'm not ready. Besides, I have bigger plans. Although..." Doug stopped at a crosswalk waiting for the light to change.

"Although what?" Victor felt his heart racing and his mouth getting dryer by the moment.

Doug laughed and shook his head. "Just something my dad always said," he glanced over at Victor. "He always used to say, '*there's money in them walls*'."

"Money in them walls," Victor mumbled rubbing his chin. "Money in them walls," he repeated slowly. He shoved his right hand deep into his cargo shorts pocket and tightened his grip on a knife he'd lifted off a homeless guy outside of The Mission.

"What do you mean? He has, like, cash stashed inside the walls of the bar?" Victor imagined himself floating in a pool of cash, on a drug high. "How much money?"

"Naw, it's not like that." Doug stepped off the curb as the light changed and the two walked another block together until they reached an alley.

"Hey, Doug, over here," Victor said as he stepped into the alley and motioned for Doug to follow him. The young man stood for a moment with his brow furrowed, staring at Victor. "I just gotta' take a piss, but I wanted to tell you about...what I found in your dad's..." Victor's heart was racing. He needed to get that money. "Come on, man, like, I'll only take a second."

"What did you find? What are you talking about?" Doug inched his way into the alley.

"Hold on," Victor said standing behind a dumpster. A rush of air swept through the dark alley picking up the sour and rancid smells from the trash.
In a swift motion, Victor pulled the knife out of his shorts pocket. He just wanted the money. He didn't expect Doug to lunge at him. The college boy dropped to the filthy pavement beside the dumpster. And as the blood ran from his body, Victor snatched his wallet, backpack, and pulled the loose money out of the young man's pocket. He threw the knife in the dumpster and looked around again to make sure no one saw him.

Everything felt frantic, fast, and exciting. He sucked in deep breaths like a swimmer coming up for air. Victor wedged Doug's body between the brick wall and the dumpster, where it lay hidden from the single light bulb above an alley door. Victor laughed uncontrollably, anxiously and ran.

The handful of money would only get him one fix, maybe two. He needed more.

Victor Nellis was still a desperate man.

CHAPTER TWO

The October storm howled from the north into Whisper Creek, Idaho. Rain splatted against the windows. Tazia Drake shot up from a deep sleep at the sound of a limb crashing against the side of the house. She rolled over and sat on the edge of her bed, caught her breath while remnants of a dream slipped through her mind.

A woman in the shadows. A black cat with burning green eyes.

Pushing her long hair back out of her face, Tazia got up and watched out the window. The porch light was out. The streetlight was out too. The city was blanketed in darkness. Rainwater, her large black and white cat, peeked out from under the bed.

"It's okay, Rainwater." Tazia grabbed the robe off the foot of her bed and ambled into the bathroom. "It's just the wind. Sounds like a limb broke off the tree." The house was dark, the power was out, but at least Grandmother was still asleep. She got a drink of water and returned to bed. Something in her dream tugged at her as she snuggled under the blankets and fell back to sleep.

It was still dark outside when the alarm on her cell phone buzzed at five-thirty Friday morning. It was cold in the room and she didn't want to leave her warm bed. Tazia hit the snooze button. Ten minutes later the alarm went off again. She reached for the snooze a second time but changed her mind. She turned the alarm off and sat up, stretching and yawning. Why did morning have to come so early? The numbers on her electric alarm clock flashed telling her the power was back on. She reset the clocks, had a quick breakfast and was off to work.

Sitting at her desk in the news room, Tazia scanned websites searching for a story to write. It was a slow news week in the rural town of Whisper Creek. Her cell phone pinged with a text message. She picked up the phone, swiped it to read.

Leslie: *You free for a drink after work? You won't believe what Chuck and I just did.*

Tazia: *Sure, how about the Neon Moon at 4:30?*

Leslie: *Great, see you then.*

Leslie Brodie and Tazia had been friends since third grade. The day Leslie arrived in the classroom with little splotches of blood all over her new yellow sweater. Apparently she'd picked up an injured squirrel on the way to school and they'd had a difference of opinions. It seemed the squirrel won, but Tazia thought carrying a squirrel was really cool, although she didn't know if the blood stains were Leslie's or the squirrel's. She admired the scrawny blond girl from that day on.

Tazia stared out the office window. It was one of those wretched afternoons when nothing could penetrate the grey sky or her equally grey mood. She hated slow news days. *I need a story. What's a newspaper with no news?* She opened a drawer and rummaged through old files to find an idea she could bring to life.

"Drake," Curtis, her boss barked from across the newsroom. "What are you working on?"

"Whether I should be a Cubs ballplayer or a pirate for Halloween this year."

Curtis stood with hands on his broad hips and glared at her.

"What do you think?" Tazia smirked at her boss.

"I think you better start writing or you'll be dressing up as an out-of-work reporter for Halloween."

"Actually, I'm working on a soft piece right now, plans by the City Council for the upcoming fall street fair." She waited for a response, but the publisher waved and mumbled then retreated back to his office. Typical.

At ten minutes past four, Tazia rapidly tapped her pencil on the edge of her desk. Scouring websites had turned up little, and certainly nothing of interest.

Eight boring, frustrating, unproductive hours she spent on the police tweet decks following all their posts, Facebook, Twitter, the court sites, the county sites, and the city's. She tossed the pencil in her drawer, turned off her computer and headed to meet her friend.

Only a handful of people occupied The Neon Moon Bar and Grill at four-thirty on Friday afternoon. It was the usual crowd for this time of day. Marty and Josh racked up the balls on the pool table. Cheryl and Cathy ordered their usual at the end of the counter to go over the day's work. Better at The Neon Moon than the real estate office. Tazia ordered her usual Miller Lite and a whiskey for Leslie, and scooted into the corner booth. She scrolled through messages on her cell phone while waiting for her friend.

Leslie was a skinny blond who always looked like she'd just finished running a marathon, with her shoulder-length messy hair sticking out in different directions, no makeup except for traces of faded lipstick. She slid into the booth huffing out of breath, but Tazia knew it was from her nicotine habit, and not running any race. The only actual running Leslie did was from one project to the next.

The waiter set a whiskey on the table in front of Leslie and the beer in front of Tazia. "Will there be anything else ladies? Appetizers?"

"Not right now, thanks," Leslie quickly grabbed her glass and took a sip. She looked at Tazia,

"As you know, Chuck's always looking for our next project, and well…we found one."

"Not another B and B in Cuba, I hope," Tazia leaned forward and chuckled at the failed plans her friends had the year before. That had been a yearlong fiasco that just about destroyed Chuck and Leslie's marriage.

"Even better," Leslie smirked.

"Do tell," Tazia smiled and viewed her cell phone out of habit. Maybe she would have a story after all.

"We just bought the Casino. It's a bar and hotel in Ketchum. Although it's not really a hotel anymore, hasn't been for a long time. But the bar's been running consistently since it opened in the mid 1920's."

"Ketchum's not on a reservation, how can you have a casino there?"

"No, that's just the name. Actually, when the place was first built, it was a boarding house for miners and gambling was legal then. So at one time it was an actual casino. The gambling is gone, but the name stuck."

"When did you buy it?"

"Um, we bought it…I guess it was mid-August."

"And you're just now telling me about it?"

"Yes, but you're still first. We haven't told anyone down here about it yet. You know how our projects go. Sometimes they pan out and sometimes they don't. But so far, this is going really great. Anyway, I've been up there for the past month working on the place and just got back yesterday."

"What are you going to do with a bar in Ketchum?"

"What every bar owner does – sell drinks and make money!" Leslie gave a sheepish grin and took another drink of her whiskey. "This place is fabulous. The building's on the historical register and it has way more charm than any of the new structures in town. And get this… it's *haunted*."

Tazia nearly knocked her beer over. "Haunted? Seriously? How do you know?"

"Everyone knows. I haven't seen the ghost yet, but a couple of our bartenders have. I'm gonna' head back up tomorrow. There's so much work that still needs to be done. Our first goal's to remodel the side space and open a little café. There's an original barber shop that's part of the building too. You'll love the barber; he's been there for eons! And then there's…well, just so much."

"At least I don't have to have a passport to get there, right?" Tazia laughed. "What is that, a three hour drive from here?"

"If the roads are good. But yeah, depending on weather and traffic. Come up, spend a few days with me. You can help me do some planning. I'd love to remodel the upstairs at some point and open the hotel again."

"How big is the hotel?"

"Not big at all. Only fifteen rooms and they're super tiny. But there's potential, you know? I think I'd like to make it more of a boarding house again, maybe for local workers. Something that the community really needs. I mean, the area already has more than enough for the rich and famous. But the Casino is for the locals."

"You're heading up tomorrow, huh?" The thought sent a sudden rush of goosebumps through Tazia's arms, a sensation she got when she was on the precipice of something great. The ideas were spinning in her brain like a pinwheel. A renovation of a historical building wasn't a top story, but it was a story. She could play around with that. What really intrigued her was the ghost. "I'm sure Grandmother wouldn't mind me being gone for a few days. Let me see what Curtis thinks."

"That would be awesome if he'd put a story about our bar in the Herald. And I could definitely use your help getting things ready. Our grand opening's a week from tomorrow." Leslie took another drink of her whiskey. "No pressure!" she said in a tense high-pitched voice.

"Count me in, Les," Tazia picked up her phone and opened the text message string with her boss. "I'll embellish a little to get his okay. If he doesn't approve, I'll just take a week's vacation."

The last time Tazia took a vacation was three years earlier when she and her sister, Lainey, took her nieces to Disneyland. With two little girls constantly wanting to go in opposite directions, and a big sister complaining about everything Tazia did, it took her a month to recover. A vacation on her own was blossoming in her mind with the sweetness of Grandmother's white sage smudges.

They ordered another round of drinks along with a large plate of nachos. The two friends toasted to the new haunted acquisition as the sky outside bruised into night.

CHAPTER THREE

On Saturday morning Tazia drove to the office to tie up some loose ends at work. She had two mediocre stories that could run while she was gone, so she queued them into the system. Curtis, the publisher, would decide where and when he wanted to run them. Then she hurried home to pack two suitcases. A big one for clothes and a smaller one with writing essentials – laptop, charging cords, notebooks, snacks.

Who knew how long she would be up there? If it was fun and there was a promising story, she might last the full week. If not, she'd probably only stay a few days. Tazia had a tendency to get bored easily. Her fluffy cat kept walking across the open bag on the bed as Tazia folded clothes and neatly tucked them in. "Rainwater, I can't take you, and I don't want to take all your shedding hair with me either. Scooch!" She shooed the cat to the side of the bed. Rainwater meowed and slowly inched his way back to the edge of the suitcase.

Pulling on her Chicago Cubs ball cap, Tazia reached for the leather pouch hanging around her neck. The medicine bundle Grandmother had given her last summer. She knew it was nothing more than feathers, crystals and sage, but it felt like an unseen protector, a guardian watching over her. She felt an unexplainable sense of safety when wearing her ball cap and medicine bundle. If she believed in luck or superstition, these were her two lucky charms.

A dull feeling gnawed at the pit of her stomach as she zipped up the two suitcases. Tazia reached over to close the blinds on her bedroom window and jumped back startled. A woman in black stood outside her window staring in at her. She looked again, but the woman had disappeared. She pressed her face to the glass and looked around the yard as far as she could see, but the woman was gone. Had she imagined it? Absently, her hand cradled the medicine bundle for comfort.

A hint of danger remained like an aftertaste from last night's dream. A woman in the shadows. Death. Not once, but twice. What was she going to find in Ketchum?

Tazia pulled her rolling suitcases into the living room. Grandmother sat nestled in her brown leather recliner with an afghan on her lap, a book in her hands, and a steaming cup of coffee on the table beside her. The fireplace cast a warm orange glow across the elder's face. The smell of burning pine logs filled the room rising with the warm air toward the loft upstairs.

"I'm ready to leave," Tazia said in her native Sioux. "You can call me anytime if you need anything. And Lainey's available to help out too." Grandmother folded down the corner of the page she was reading and laid the book in her lap.

"She waits for you," Grandmother murmured in her native Sioux language.

"Who?"

"The lady in the shadows. The woman who remains as only a memory. But she is still there, and she waits for you." She looked up at Tazia with a mischievous grin on her lips. "Are you taking my Grandson with you?"

"Grandmother!" Tazia scoffed. "Matteo Alfieri is not your Grandson! And he is definitely not my boyfriend! He's a friend, that's it, and you know it." She leaned over the old woman and kissed her on the forehead. "So you can stop your wishful thinking." Tazia smiled, wondering who was wishing for the relationship more, Grandmother or her? "I'm going to help Leslie and Chuck with the grand opening of the bar they bought." And hopefully, Tazia added to herself, I can get Agent Alfieri out of my head for a few days.

Grandmother wiggled a little farther back into her chair. "Not good time for business opening. *Canwape Kasna Wi*," she said. Moon of the changing leaves. "Be careful, danger hides in the shadow of change."

Tazia glanced at her cell phone, then back at Grandmother. "You're too superstitious, Grandmother. October's my favorite time of the year. Not too hot, not too cold. I love watching all the leaves change color and fall through the air." Tazia stepped close to the crackling fireplace and typed a text on her phone. Sliding the phone in her pocket, she smiled at Grandmother. "I love you, and I'll call you when I get there." She grabbed a suitcase handle with each hand and rolled toward the door.

"*KahápA tókha šni*," Grandmother whispered. Drive safely.

Tazia blew her grandmother a kiss and gently closed the door behind her. She slid the two small suitcases into the back seat of her Mini Cooper and finished the text message on her phone.

TAZIA: Leaving Whisper Creek now, see you in about three hours.

She plugged the phone in to the charger cable, set the radio to her favorite contemporary country music station and headed east to the mountains.

"I have a week off," Tazia said aloud, surprised at how good that felt. She never liked being away from Grandmother for more than a day. In a sense, Grandmother had become her life preserver; she kept Tazia from drowning in the darkness after her husband died. Killed in the line of duty, they said. Ha! Tazia snorted. Simon's duty was to stay with her, raise a family, and grow old together. But that didn't happen. Instead, at the age of thirty, Tazia was a widow. Grandmother filled the empty echoes in Tazia's home by moving in shortly after Simon's death. The Sioux medicine woman was exactly what Tazia's shattered heart needed, although, she wasn't about to admit that to anyone. She smiled at the thought and turned up the radio to sing along to a Keith Urban song, *Blue Ain't Your Color*.

It was a quiet drive on the interstate past the city of Boise, through the dry sagebrush covered plains to Mountain Home, and left into the Sawtooth National Forest area and the Wood River Valley. She was starting to adjust to the idea of this little get-away. Her sister, Lainey, was always badgering her about being a work-a-holic.

Ketchum's beauty and rich color brightened Tazia's eyes and made her smile. She hadn't been up this way for years. She wasn't much of a winter and snow person, so Tazia stayed away from the little mountain town that was one of the oldest and most elite ski resorts in America. A place where Hollywood stars came to escape the paparazzi. But Tazia wasn't going there to catch a glimpse of Mariel Hemingway or Tom Hanks, she was going to a place that catered to locals.

And ghosts.

CHAPTER FOUR

The Sawtooth Mountains were cloaked in autumn colors as Tazia crested the mountain road and eased down into the small town nestled in the valley. The outside temperature had dropped from sixty to fifty degrees giving the air a sudden chill. She relaxed as she drove the tree-lined streets blanketed in gold and crimson leaves. Finally, she parked in front of the Casino bar then stood on the sidewalk inhaling the crisp clean air. No smog or inversion here. She grabbed her purse from the passenger seat, locked the Mini Cooper, and headed into the bar. She stopped to read the bronze plaque next to the door, KETCHUM KAMP HOTEL, BUILT 1925, KETCHUM-SUN VALLY HISTORICAL SOCIETY. It seemed Leslie and Chuck had a stroke of luck catching this place on the market.

It was almost three o'clock in the afternoon and the bar was empty except for one bartender. The mid-fifties man with brown hair, an approachable smile and a white cotton apron wrapped around his waist, moved effortlessly behind the bar sliding glasses onto racks and shelves. He whistled along with the music that played over the sound system. A song Tazia knew well, *It's 5 O'clock Somewhere.*

"Hi, I'm Tazia Drake." She offered a friendly smile. "Is Leslie around?"

The bartender looked up with a gleam in his eye and a welcoming grin on his face. "You bet," he wiped his hands on his apron and reached out to shake. "I'm Dave. Have a seat. I'll get her for you. Want anything while you wait?"

"No thanks," Tazia shook her head. Dave strolled to the end of the bar and looked around the corner into the kitchen area.

"Hey boss, you got someone out here lookin' for ya." Dave leaned back toward Tazia. "Sure I can't get you something? I make a mean margarita!"

A margarita did sound good. "Sold. Blended, no salt, please."

"You got it," Dave pulled down a bottle of tequila and poured a shot into the blender.

"That drink's on me, Dave," Leslie said as she stepped into the bar from the kitchen. "In fact, anything Taz has while she's here is on me." She scooted around the corner of the bar and gave Tazia a big hug. "I'm so glad you made it, I'm beyond stressed. Get your drink and I'll give you the tour."

The bar was old with large timbers visible in the low ceiling and walls. It was clear the place hadn't been updated in ages. The hard wood floor had grooves from years of traffic, the lighting was dim in older fixtures and the bar itself was worn and discolored with age. "This was a popular haunt of Ernest Hemingway in the day," Leslie said pointing to a black and white photo of Hemingway with buddies sitting at the bar, drinking and laughing.

"Isn't this the last place he lived?" Tazia asked scooping up her blended drink and taking a sip. "Hemingway? Yes, an unfortunate end to an amazing man. Come on," Leslie pointed to the large round timbers. "The historic nature of the building is important, and Chuck's adamant about keeping that intact."

"I don't blame him."

"This building was originally constructed from logs chopped and hauled down from Bald Mountain." Leslie looked at Tazia. "Maybe you can write an article for the grand opening with some of that in it?" They walked across the hardwood floor opposite of the bar to a door marked *Authorized Personnel Only.*

"You mentioned it was a real casino at one time. Like legal gambling?"

"Oh yeah," Leslie opened the door and walked into a short hallway with one door to the left and one to the right. Stairs straight ahead led up to the second floor. She opened the door on the right first, exposing a large pantry with wall-to-wall, floor-to-ceiling shelves that held every kind of liquor. Each row was six bottles deep.

"The original owners bought this place the same year that the Union Pacific Railroad opened the Sun Valley Resort. Legalized gambling in the 1930s consisted of mostly card games. Poker and black jack. That's when the property got named the Ketchum Kamp Hotel and Casino. Then, when gambling was outlawed in the early fifties it became just a bar."

Leslie closed the liquor room door and opened the door across from it. She entered and waved her hand like a model presenting a game show lineup. "But after the legal gambling shut down, this room became a private poker room with some pretty high-stake games. Now it's just a storage room."

Stepping back into the short hallway, Leslie led Tazia up the old narrow staircase to the second floor. At the top of the stairs and the front of the building was an office on the left side of the hall and a bedroom and bathroom were on the right. "This is our office, but you can feel free to use it while you're here." Leslie looked around the cluttered room of mismatched furniture, an old wood desk, a tall metal filing cabinet and a worn couch. "And this room across the hall is where you can stay, if you're okay staying here?"

Tazia gazed around the room at the double bed, small desk and a couple of chairs. It looked like it had been decorated by a college kid, no bed frame, more mismatched furniture that looked like it came from the second-hand store, a small fridge with a microwave sitting on top. "Sure, are you kidding? I'd be happy to crash here."

"Chuck and I live in a small one-bedroom cottage behind the building when we're up here. And for Chuck, that's most of the time. Come on, there's more to see." Leslie motioned for Tazia to follow her out into the narrow dim hall. "Like I said, it hasn't been a hotel in years, as you can tell, and wouldn't meet code for that now, anyway."

"What are you going to do with it?" Tazia stopped for a moment in each doorway of the thirteen other rooms on the second floor. They were tiny in size, barely big enough for a single bed and a nightstand.

"It started as a boarding house. That's kinda what I've been thinking, making it something along that line again."

The two friends made their way to the far end of the hall, peeking in each room as they went. Tazia took a picture of a couple of the rooms with her cell phone. Renovations barely underway revealed lathe and cracked plaster walls peeking out from ripped and drooping faded floral wallpaper. She snapped pictures of the rooms Chuck had been working on with new sheetrock and plaster on the walls, ripped and worn linoleum replaced and one room was even painted a nice soft eggshell white. The last room they looked at was a work-in-progress with new sheetrock on the walls and piles of old brittle wallpaper heaped on the floor.

"Wow," Tazia sighed. "You've still got a lot of work to do. When's your grand opening?"

"Ha!" Leslie chuckled and ran a dust-covered hand through her curly hair. "Next Saturday, one week from today. But that's only for the bar downstairs. It'll be a year or more, probably a lot more, before we open the upstairs to the public. Come on, there's still the third floor."

The pair ventured up the creaky wood stairs to the third floor, which was one large open room with a vaulted ceiling. There was one window at each end of the room, and a single lightbulb that hung from a cord over the top of the stairs. The smell of dust and age was overpowering. Tazia rubbed her nose and held back a sneeze. "This was the real boarding area. Miners would come to town and pay for a twin bed in here, which included a hot meal and a drink downstairs. But I don't think I'll ever open the third floor to the public."

"So what will you use it for?" Tazia stood next to the railing of the stairs and peered into the dark expanse that extended the length of the building. A cold draft brushed the old timbers of the high ceiling. "It would make a great private room, like for entertaining. It's huge." Tazia's voice echoed across the vastness of the third floor.

"It would, but can you imagine navigating those stairs after a few drinks?"

"You do have a point there. Better make the couches up here all futons or hide-a-beds." Tazia chuckled. "Just put in some better lighting, a huge TV, a small wet bar, and a bunch of couches and you have the perfect private party room."

Tazia moved into the shadowy third floor. She stopped mid-stride at the sound of a rustle in the far corner. It was too dark to see across to the other side. She felt for the cell phone in her pocket and gulped. Even the flashlight app on her phone wasn't enough light for the space. She could sense a presence. Something other worldly, existing in the dark.

Stepping back, Tazia slowly scanned the open space with her light. She didn't see anything, but sensed something was there. Someone-*she* was there. The woman in her dream. The woman Grandmother told her about. Tazia quickly returned to Leslie.

"This floor needs the most work, but I do like your ideas," Leslie murmured. "But then… there's the ghost."

"The what?" Tazia felt edgy.

"The ghost. Remember, I told you this place is haunted."

Tazia sucked in a shaky breath and reached out for the railing around the stairs. "Is the second floor haunted too? Where I'm going to be staying?" She could hear the anxiety in her own voice.

"Don't worry, she's not evil. And besides, Chuck and I've been in here for a few months now and we haven't seen anything." Leslie walked to the window near the stairs that overlooked the main street in the front of the building. "If you're not comfortable staying here, I'll pay for a hotel room in Hailey."

"No, no," Tazia said as she started down the stairs back to the second floor, her white knuckles gripping the railing. "I'm sure I'll be fine. I really want to hang out with the people in the bar and get to know everyone. I think a story on this place is a great idea."

"Wait 'til you meet Paul." They strolled down the narrow hallway and back to the office on the second floor. Leslie cleared some papers off the corner of the desk and piled them on top of the filing cabinet. "Paul'll be in around ten tomorrow morning; I can't wait for you to meet him."

"Another bartender?" Tazia slumped into the sagging couch at the end of the desk as Leslie sat down and logged onto her computer.

"No, Paul's the barber. You saw the barber shop on the front of the building next to the front door? It's been part of this building from the beginning. The guy doesn't look it, but he's got to be in his eighties." Leslie lit a cigarette and took a drag, then set it in the ashtray on the desk as she looked back at the computer screen.

"You sure this place is haunted? I mean, like, a *real* ghost?" Tazia asked twirling her long raven black hair in her fingers almost to the point of being tangled. Muffled sounds from the bar rose through the aged timbers. Lively. Music. Laughter. Voices.

"Hold on," Leslie mumbled as she scrolled through some emails and took another drag from her cigarette letting the smoke swirl around her. She typed a few responses, then logged off and turned around to face Tazia. "Maybe it's haunted, maybe it's not. There's stories, right? This building is old and every old building has stories. I can tell you that the bartenders refuse to be alone in here at night after closing."

"And you want me to stay up here alone? Maybe I better take the room in Hailey," Tazia said with wide eyes. "I don't do so good with ghosts." She cocked her head a little at a strange sound that caught her attention. "What was that?"

"What?" Leslie asked.

"I thought…nothing. Never mind."

"No, what? Did you hear something?"

"I thought…I thought I heard a whisper. I'm sure it was just the wind through these old walls."

"You're just being paranoid now," Leslie laughed nervously and stood up. "Come on, let's go talk to Dave. Brent should be down there too."

"Brent?" Tazia stood up with Leslie.

"He's another one of our bartenders," Leslie said, taking one last drag off of her cigarette and rubbing it out in the ashtray.

"How many bartenders do you have?"

"Enough to keep this place running so I don't have to worry about things. Come on."

The two made their way down the narrow stairs and back to the main bar area.

"How's that margarita?" Dave called out to Tazia. "Ready for a refill?"

Tazia strolled over to the bar and slid her empty glass toward him. "I think I'll wait on the refill. Gotta' pace myself, you know?" She chuckled. "Hey Dave, you ever see a ghost here?"

Wiping some clean glasses before putting them on the shelf, Dave didn't skip a beat. "You bet, saw a ghost of a little girl plain as you and me, one day. I was in there filling up an ice bucket and turned to see her standing right beside me. At first I thought she was some kid who wandered in off the street, ya' know? Except she was dressed funny, like a below-the-knee skirt and button-up blouse. Pretty blond ringlets, and she stared at me with the strangest expression, didn't say a word. And then she was gone. Like, vanished. It was really freaky."

"I saw the lady. I think it was the ghost of Slavey's wife," Brent chimed in as he checked off items on a sheet of paper, matching inventory of the liquor bottles on the shelves. He turned and held his hand out, "Hi, I'm Brent, the fastest bartender in Ketchum. You ever see the movie *Cocktail* with Tom Cruise?"

Tazia furrowed her brow for a moment trying to remember. "Oh yeah, the bartenders."

"That's me! Haven't been here quite as long as Dave, but almost." He was five foot eight to Dave's six foot one. Brent was wiry with brown curly hair, black rimmed glasses and a square jaw. He had dark blue eyes the color of denim.

"How long have you been a bartender here?" Tazia asked.

"Thirty-one years," said Dave.

"I've been here twelve. This place's like that *Cheers* on TV. The tourists pack the place next door and across the street, but the locals come here.

"Tell me about the lady ghost you saw," Tazia opened her little notebook. "Who's Slavey?"

"Slavey used to own this place back in the beginning. He died upstairs in the late forties. But his wife, Dora, she continued to live here until she died in the eighties. In fact she slept in that room over there, the old poker room." Brent pointed to the door that led to the storage rooms. "That was Dora's bedroom until she was way into her nineties. I understand she was a heck of a woman too. Everyone in town loved her. She had the brain for business, ya know? Smart. Didn't take no crap from anyone, but would help any of those who needed it." Brent flipped the page on his checklist.

"And you saw her ghost?"

"I think so," Brent laid the pencil down on the paper and pushed his glasses up into his hairline. "I mean, I saw a woman in a long dress. She walked right past me when I was taking inventory in the storage room. She went up the stairs, but when I looked up there she was gone. I really didn't want to go up the stairs to find out where she went." Brent shivered as if he was cold. "I make sure I'm never here alone though, that's for sure."

"Is she scary?" Tazia pressed.

"No, not really. I mean, other than it's just freaky to see a ghost. Someone who's not really there, ya' know?" Brent let out a nervous laugh. "And I don't really want to take the chance of it getting…I don't know…evil?" He rubbed his brow. "Maybe I watch too many horror movies. But ghosts just make me uncomfortable." He picked the pencil back up.

"Hey hon, I'm done here for the day. Heading to the store then I'll be in the cabin. You need anything?" Chuck said stepping out of the kitchen brushing dust off his jeans.

"No, I'm good. You want to stick around for a drink with us?"

"Naw," Chuck leaned over and kissed his wife on the cheek. "I need a hot shower and besides, I have a bottle of Jack in the cabin."

Tazia waved to Chuck, jotted down a few more notes, then scooted to the end of the bar where Leslie stood. Tazia slid her notebook into her jacket pocket. "How's this, I'll stay here during the day. I can work upstairs in the office on my laptop and hang out down here getting to know everyone in the evenings, but I think I'll sleep in a hotel. Not really comfortable being the only person in the building after the bar shuts down."

"No problem," Leslie said as she pulled out her cell phone. "Although, if you weren't too fussy, you could sleep on the couch in our cabin behind the Casino. It's small, but cozy, and the couch is actually more comfortable than our bed."

Dave threw the bar towel over his shoulder and smiled. "I'd take the couch."

"What do you think?" Leslie looked at Tazia. They both shrugged their shoulders.

"I'm good with a comfy couch. Thanks." With that settled, Tazia's stomach rumbled loud enough for her friend to hear.

"Good, let's go get some dinner and discuss the week's plan," Leslie said. She reached around the corner and grabbed her coat and stocking hat. "Come on, dinner's on me."

The two left the bar and walked across the street to Whiskey Jacques.

CHAPTER FIVE

The next morning Tazia awoke to Leslie and Chuck milling around the kitchen of the small cabin. She heard dishes clinking and the smell of fresh brewed coffee brushed her senses. A dark French roast. Their conversation and laughter filtered into the living room.

Tazia sat up on the couch, grabbed her jeans and Chicago Cubs sweatshirt and headed to the bathroom to get dressed. She brushed her long black hair as bits of a dream from the night before unfolded in her mind. She gathered her blankets and piled her bedding on the end of the couch. She thought about the dream, it was a repeat of one she'd had at home the past couple of nights. The woman in the shadows. Blood. A black cat.

"Good morning, sunshine," Leslie said in a sing-song voice cradling a cup of coffee in her hands. Tazia shuffled into the kitchen, noticeably warmed by the oven and two smiling faces. "Coffee's ready if you want. Sugar and creamer are on the counter. I have cream cheese for bagels. There's plenty of eggs and bacon in the fridge too. Help yourself to whatever you want."

"Thanks," Tazia yawned and pulled a coffee cup off the shelf. "This is all I need right now." She sat down at the small drop-leaf table beside the window. Chuck sat across from her drinking his coffee with his face buried in the morning paper.

"You okay?" Leslie asked.

"Sure, just not awake yet. This is me pre-caffeine. Why?" Tazia mumbled.

"You look like something's troubling you."

Chuck glanced up from the paper he was reading. "If the couch isn't a good sleep, we can get you a hotel room."

"No," Tazia said. "The couch is great. I slept fine. Just a…" she looked at Leslie's and Chuck's attentive eyes waiting for her explanation. "Just an odd dream that's bugging me. That's all."

"I'm on my way to the store, so take your time with breakfast." Leslie finished her coffee and headed into the living room.

The toaster popped up with two bagels and Chuck dropped the paper on the table and pulled the bagel pieces out and laid them on a plate. "Toasted bagels. Want one?" The smell lingered in the tiny cabin and made her stomach growl.

"Mmmm, " Tazia said nodding and sniffing the aromas.

After they ate and drank their coffee, Chuck folded up his newspaper and put the dirty dishes in the sink. He pulled his jacket off the coat rack near the door and zipped it up. "I'll be working in the kitchen area of the bar if you need me," he said.

Tazia looked at her watch. Ten a.m. She gathered up her things and pulled on her parka. "I'm going to walk around for a bit then I'll be over there." She pulled her long hair through the opening in the back of her Cubs baseball cap. "Shouldn't be more than an hour or so."

"Take your time. After all, you're our guest," Chuck said as he slid his cell phone in his pocket and stepped out the door.

It was a clear morning but cold enough that Tazia could see her breath. She shoved her hands deep in her coat pockets and headed down to Starbucks first. She loved Leslie's coffee, but it was no contender against a mocha latte. The Starbucks was inside the Ketchum Visitor's Center, which offered a whole wall of brochures, flyers, and magazines on the area. Tazia grabbed a couple of magazines and sat in the corner beside a large window with her mocha. She smiled on a deep inhale of the mocha fragrance, and perused the local literature. She stopped for a moment and watched the people as they passed by on the charming streets of the small town. There was a definite charm to this area that resonated with her. She had never really spent any time in the Wood River Valley before, something she realized she would have to change. This was a magical place. After a stroll past the quaint gift shops and small up-scale boutiques, she headed back to her friend's bar.

The Casino was empty except for Tazia and Dave behind the bar. She sat at the end of the bar, her Starbucks cup in front of her as she read through her notes. She tried to figure out a way to pitch a story to Curtis that he would approve for the Herald. Her publisher normally liked news that was local, but if it had appeal and was a good story, he was usually open to it. She let out a sigh and scratched out another idea she knew wouldn't fly. She needed a twist for the article to stand out. Leslie arrived an hour later and put her purse behind the bar and wrapped a white apron around her waist.

"It's going to be a busy day, you sure you want to help? If you need to work, you're more than welcome to hang out upstairs and work on your computer. The Wi-Fi password is on a sticky note on the back of my monitor up there." Leslie went into the kitchen between the bar and the small café on the other side. "I'm putting on a pot of coffee, want a refill?" she called out to Tazia.

"No thanks, I think I've had my limit today," Tazia called back. She turned around and leaned against the bar, gazing slowly at the room. Hardwood floor. Three pool tables. A foosball table. Some tables and chairs for seating scattered around the room. The interior walls were all log, no doubt original. There was even an old wooden phone booth with a seat in it, but no phone. There was a new digital juke box for music and several flat screen TVs mounted on the walls. The building had aged well and was in good shape.

"I think Paul's in," Leslie set her coffee cup down on the counter and nodded to the door at the end of the bar that led into the barber shop.

"Great," Tazia said sliding her purse strap over her shoulder. They strolled into the small room that housed two barber chairs. One sink sat in a short counter in front of a mirror that covered the entire back wall. The barber chair in front of the window was an obvious antique. Its shiny aged leather seat edged with ornate decorative silver framing. The other chair sat in the middle of the room with a leather strap for sharpening razor blades. Paul was a traditional man.

"Hey Paul, this is my friend, Tazia Drake that I told you about. She's a reporter for the Herald in Moon County."

Paul gave a friendly nod and smile as he extended his hand to Tazia. He didn't look as old as Leslie had suggested. His grey-brown hair wasn't even thinning yet. His goatee, however, did have more grey in it. His soft brown eyes glimmered behind his black rimmed glasses. Paul's tee shirt that sported classic cars on it was neatly tucked in to his pressed denim jeans, synched by an old weathered brown belt. He was taller than Tazia, but only by a few inches. He had a round belly but not overly large, and he looked to Tazia as if he was maybe in his early sixties. Surely Leslie had been mistaken saying he was near eighty years old. But Paul assured her, he was indeed, seventy-nine.

"Hi, I'd love to do a little piece on your barber shop. Is that okay with you?" Tazia took out her cell phone.

"You can write whatever size of piece you want," Paul laughed. "I'm all yours 'til a customer comes in."

"Thanks," Tazia said and snapped a few pictures with her phone, then turned on the recorder app. "Tell me about this place."

Paul leaned against the back of the main barber chair, crossed his arms over his chest and smiled as his eyes swept over the many historical black and white photos that covered the walls. "Well there's not much to tell. I'm just a barber."

Tazia glanced around the room at the history of the town proudly displayed on the walls. "It looks to me like there's a lot to tell. I'd love to hear it."

"Well, let's see," Paul rubbed his chin. "I moved up here in 1964, and I've been barbering in this spot for fifty-five years. I've been in the business for fifty-eight years."

Tazia stared at him for a moment in amazement. He certainly didn't look his age. "Do you have any employees?"

Paul shook his head no. "No, this is a one-man shop."

"Thinking of retiring soon?" Tazia asked as she jotted a few notes in her small notebook.

"Heck, I can't retire. I'll work here 'til I drop." Paul chuckled.

"I know this is an old building, and some say it's haunted. In fact, Dave, one of the bartenders, said he saw a ghost in the bar." Tazia looked up at Leslie and winked. "Paul, have you ever seen a ghost here?"

"I don't think I ever drank that much." Paul shook his head and laughed. He had a friendly laugh that made her feel comfortable and welcome. "This business has been good to me. I like giving a man a smart cut and a clean shave."

"You ever cut women's hair?" Tazia raised an eyebrow at him.

"No. Well there was that one exception when the actress Demi Moore was doing the movie G.I. Jane. I did cut her hair for that." Paul laughed and explained how Bruce Willis was one of his most loyal clients. He went on to talk about Slavey, the building's long-time owner, the other businesses that came and went in town, and all the colorful history as he pointed to the photos that lined the walls, telling the story of each one. The people and the businesses of the small town of Ketchum, all captured and hanging on Paul Webster's barber shop walls.

They finished the interview with Paul and headed back into the bar. It was early afternoon and a couple of people were sitting along the bar, talking and having a beer. A young woman stomped across the hard wood floor in her two-inch heeled boots, her heavy footsteps echoed in the large room. She looked to be in her early twenties. But after being so wrong with Paul's age, Tazia didn't trust her guesses on age anymore. The young lady tramped up to the bar like she owned the town, wearing unflattering polka dot leggings and a cherry red fleece pullover.

"Hey Leslie, I heard you have a news reporter from the valley up here?" the gal said with a tone of dissatisfaction in her voice.

"I'm Tazia Drake with the Herald in Moon County. And you are?"

"Claire Chandler with the Mountain Messenger. *I* cover all the news here. We really don't need your help," Claire huffed. She was clearly marking her territory. She was heavy-chested, wide across the top of her body with a flat butt and skinny hips and legs. She looked like a funnel with tight curly brown hair on the top. It was an odd picture that formed in Tazia's mind.

"I'm not the competition, Claire. I'm here to help my friend with the grand opening of her bar."

Tazia tried to hold her tongue and not mark her own territory. After all, she was a guest up here.

"How long are you in town for?" Claire demanded with narrowing eyes.

"Undetermined at this point," Tazia said as calmly as she could, but it wasn't easy. The funnel-girl was pissing her off. "I haven't decided yet. I rather like it up here. Not a bad place for an award-winning journalist like myself," she spit out the words at the local reporter. Snarkiness was the order of the day for this young funnel-girl. Tazia grinned. She liked that – *funnel-girl*.

"Hmph!" Claire snorted and stomped out of the bar.

"What was that all about?" Tazia asked Leslie.

"Claire? She's just very competitive."

"Territorial's more like it," Tazia sighed. "I think I'll go upstairs and work on my notes. I need to send something to Curtis so he knows I'm still alive and well. If I can't come up with a stellar story idea, I'll just send him my vacation request and call it good." She chuckled, slipping her purse strap over her shoulder.

"There are soft drinks and bottled water in the small fridge up there. Help yourself," Leslie said as she grabbed a dish rag and wiped down the bar.

The front door opened again and a man shuffled in. He had a backpack slung over one shoulder and a lost expression on his face. Tazia stopped at the door to the stairway and turned to look at him. He ambled with a jerky movement as if unsure of where he was going. His blond hair hung down over his eyes. He was handsome with a rugged appeal, but something about him gave her an uneasy feeling.

"Hi, I'm...looking for the...owner or manager," he said with his hand outstretched to Leslie. "I'm...looking for, like, a job. My friend...Doug, said I could, like, get one here."

"I don't know a Doug, and not sure why he would tell you to come here. But, what kind of job are you looking for?" asked Leslie as she shook the man's hand.

"Doug and I...are college pals. His parents used to own this place. I understand they, like, sold it though...I'm Victor. But you can, like, call me Vic," he spoke fast with a nervous stammer to his voice which reminded Tazia of a snake oil salesman. "I'm a good...bartender, cook, like, whatever you need." Tazia noticed a slight tremble in his hands as he pushed his blond hair behind one ear. "I'm also...a gr...great handy man. I've worked on a lot of...like, remodel jobs." The young man stammered avoiding direct eye contact with anyone. Tazia noticed a fetid whiff that tinged the air and then was gone.

Tazia tightened her grip on the doorknob as she slowly turned it, still looking at the stranger. Something was off with him, she could feel it. A vision flashed through her mind for an instant. T'eíčakišwé. Death blood. What was he hiding? She opened the *Authorized Personnel Only* door and hesitated for a moment at the sound of a cat's meow drifting down the stairs. Odd, she thought, she didn't remember Leslie having a cat.

CHAPTER SIX

Tazia sat at the desk in the office above the Casino bar. She looked up from her laptop to gaze at the drizzle of rain streaming down the outside of the dormer window and mist that hung over the beautiful mountains that surrounded the small town. Even though the heater was on in the room, it felt cold to her. She wrapped her arms around herself and shivered for a moment. She thought about the fourteen empty rooms behind her, and the dark vacant third floor above her. Was there a ghost there? She felt a presence, but it didn't feel like the little girl Dave had described seeing.

When her cell phone rang she jumped, startled by the interruption. Tazia smiled at the caller ID and calmed her breathing. She picked up the phone. "Hello Agent Alf," she said, feeling warmer already. Matteo Alfieri, the FBI Agent who'd moved from New York to work with the Moon County Sheriff's office, had been the first man to truly melt her heart after her husband's death. And it seemed the more she resisted the charismatic Italian, the more she ached to be with him.

"How's my Tazmanian Devil today? And what are you up to? I heard you're out of town."

"I'm in Ketchum helping a friend out this week. She and her husband bought a business up here, and they're having a grand opening Saturday, you know, welcoming the new owners. Thought I'd write a puff piece on it. One of those feel-good stories, young couple saves aging building from destruction." Tazia chuckled.

"Was it in danger of being demolished?"

"Yes," Tazia said. "The offers they had at first were from big developers who just wanted to tear the building down and build newer and bigger, like everything else on the block. Leslie and Chuck agreed in the purchase to keep the historic building here, and to keep the staff. This place really is an icon in the area."

"I'd like to see it," Alfieri said in his husky response. She could hear a widening smile in his voice. But she knew it wasn't the building he wanted to see. It was her. That made *her* smile.

"Then you should come up on Saturday, check it out. It's a world-famous resort town. Ketchum and Sun Valley."

"I've heard of it. Even in New York we're not completely cut off from the rest of the world."

She could hear muffled conversations in the background of the call. It was clear Alfieri was still at work. "Okay," he said to someone else. "I gotta' run, but I just wanted to check in."

"I have to get back to work too. Talk to you soon." Tazia clicked off the call and set the phone down. It was easy for her to get lost in conversations with the attractive special agent. Her heart raced thinking of his grey eyes, the color of a winter sky, his thick black hair, and the smell of his earthy aftershave. She lost herself for just a moment in the memory of his muscular arms around her, his warm breath on her neck.

"Back to work," Tazia muttered to herself and returned her attention to the article she was working on. She read through what she had already written, but was interrupted again by the sound of a cat's meow. She stopped and turned, holding still to figure out where the sound was coming from. Her senses were tingling on full alert.

There it was again. The faint meow. It came from inside, but where? Tazia closed the laptop and decided to check out the place on her own. Maybe a cat had managed to get in and couldn't find its way back out. She roamed down the narrow hallway, the old floor creaking beneath her steps. She stopped to listen as she passed each of the empty rooms.

The meow continued, followed by a scratching sound. Where was the cat? The old musty air, and the curious noises set Tazia's nerves on edge. She continued down the hall but saw nothing in the rooms. She stood at the bottom of the stairs that led up to the large empty expanse of the third floor. Tazia gulped.

Meeeooow. It came again softly, more of an echo.

Something was upstairs in the attic. Tazia grasped the railing and quietly climbed the stairs. There was a large window at the top of the stairs that cast an eerie light on the landing above her. She listened to the rain patting against the roof and the windowpane.

"Here, kitty, kitty," Tazia whispered. The scratching echoed across the emptiness, seeming to come from the far side of the room blanketed in darkness. Maybe the cat was fine. If it found a way in, it would surely find its own way out. There was no way Tazia was going to walk into that opaque expanse. The thought of it felt like sinking in the depths of the ocean with no light and no air. Her breathing raced. She stepped back to the top of the stairs.

Meow.

She stopped and peered deeper into the cavernous space. Tazia felt a light sense of relief. Yes, there it was. A black cat. So black it blended in perfectly with the room, except for its green eyes that seemed to glow. The cat stopped and looked at Tazia. Both fixed in each other's gaze. The air was chilled and perfectly still.

"You shouldn't be here," Tazia whispered to the cat. A breath from somewhere in the room brushed her face.

"You shouldn't either," a voice from the darkness whispered back.

"Okay," Tazia shrieked on a brief exhale. Her eyes wide open at the emptiness of the space around her. The room exhaled a thousand sounds, but no one was there. No one she could see. Even the cat was gone. Tazia reached out for the railing and quickly inched her way back down the stairs not stopping until she was in the bar.

"I need a drink," Tazia gasped as she scooted onto a bar stool.

"What do you want?" Matt Gorby asked. He narrowed his eyes on her and tilted his head. "You look like you've seen a ghost." He wasn't joking. He knew. Gorbs had seen her too.

"Margarita on the rocks," Tazia worked at controlling her breath. "Is Leslie around?"

"She's out right now. Something about some developer giving her shit. She should be back soon." Gorbs slid the glass in front of her. "What happened?" He leaned over the bar to be closer to Tazia. He had the gentle expression of a man who understood. "You know we hear strange noises in this place all the time." He wiped the bar in front of her. "You can't help it in a place like this. I've been working here for twenty-four years, I should know." Tazia remembered now, Matt Gorby was the chatty one.

"The cat. I followed the cat to the attic," Tazia said between gasps of breath, then took a long drink.

Gorbs furrowed his brow. "There's no cat here."

Tazia pointed as she gulped down half her drink. "Upstairs, in the attic. Black cat, green eyes. And a voice."

"A voice? A talking cat?" Gorbs straightened up with a wide-eyed expression.

"No, the cat meowed then I heard a woman's voice," Tazia said.

"Damn," he shook as his whole body shivered. Gorbs looked up to the ceiling of the bar, as if he could see through the floors into the attic. "She's up there, alright."

"Who is she?" Tazia whispered.

"Don't know," Gorbs shrugged. "Some say she's Dora, one of the previous owners. She lived here until she died."

"She's the one who used to sleep in the storage room? I mean…the old poker room?" Tazia looked over her shoulder at the door across the room. Gorbs nodded, placing his elbows on the counter. "That's the one. But some say it's not her, but a woman who died here when the place was a casino. Don't know for sure. There's probably more than one ghost who haunts this old building." Gorbs looked at Tazia's now empty glass. "Want a refill?"

Holding onto her glass, Tazia thought for a moment, then slid the glass to him and nodded.

While sipping the second margarita, Tazia listened to the Zack Brown Band song that played on the juke box. The sound system in the bar was great, one of the updates Leslie and Chuck had made. Two women sat at the other end of the bar staring at one of their cell phones. They laughed, then swiped the screen, made comments, and swiped again. Tazia realized they were looking at a dating app, searching men's pictures and profiles.

Swipe, swipe, swipe.

How easy it was to disregard a person and move on to the next in a dating program. Tazia sighed. That's not how you meet the love of your life. You can't know anything from a tiny picture. Just because they can't write an interesting bio, doesn't mean *they* aren't interesting. Some people are terrible writers. She took another drink.

The front door of the Casino opened and swung shut. Leslie stomped through the small hallway from the door to the bar. She forced a smile and tossed her purse on the bar. "I'll take a Hemingway Special," she said through gritted teeth.

"What's up?" Tazia asked her friend.

"Developers. Scum. Of. The. Earth!" Leslie shook her head and glanced over at Gorbs as he made the mixed drink. "I just met with Titus Pritcher. He's pulling every damn plug he can to stop us so he can buy this place." Gorbs set the cocktail in front of Leslie and she took a swig from the glass.

"Stop you from what?" Tazia asked.

"He claims we bought this place under questionable circumstances, and that he was denied the opportunity to make an offer. He wants the block so he can tear it down and build some god-forsaken monstrosity."

"Do you own the whole block?"

"The original owners did. But they sold off half a few years back. We basically bought the other half. The Casino, the barber shop, the café, and the restaurant on the corner are all ours now." Leslie took a smaller sip of the drink and savored it for a moment. She opened her eyes and smiled at Tazia. "The only reason the owners sold to us is because we agreed *not* to tear it down. We like this place."

"Me too," Gorbs said as he turned and headed down to the other end of the bar with two Hemingway Specials in hand. He set them in front of the two ladies still going through the pictures in the dating app. Swipe.

Two men came in next, nodding at Gorbs and smiling at Tazia. "Two Coors," the taller man called out as they continued on to the pool table in the back corner. The shorter man wearing a dingy ball cap pulled a cue stick out of the rack on the wall while the taller guy racked the balls on the table. Gorbs took two cans of beer over to the table beside them and joked with the men for a minute, put the money for the drinks in his apron pocket and strolled back to the bar.

The front door opened and closed as Claire the reporter entered again. Funnel-girl. Claire stood in the entry way and scanned the room. Her eyes lit up when she saw Leslie and made a beeline to the new bar owner.

"Mrs. Brodie, I understand Titus Pritcher of TM Developers LLC is contesting your purchase of the Casino and its property. Care to comment?" The irritating funnel-girl held her cell phone in her hand, obviously with a recording app going. Tazia wondered if there was a *shut-the-bitch-up* app. She bit her lip and held back a smile.

"There's nothing to contest. We bought the property fairly and legally. Titus wanted to bulldoze down the block and build all new. We want to keep some pieces of our history intact. And that's what we're doing with the Casino."

Tazia leaned around Leslie and looked at the young reporter. "You really are writing this from the wrong angle. If you want to succeed in a small community like this, you need to take their side. Not support the outsiders."

Claire huffed her large chest and bony chin out. "I'm an excellent reporter. Certainly better than some shitty little paper like the Herald!" Claire stopped the recording app on her phone then held it up and took a picture of Leslie, then turned slightly and took a second picture of Tazia.

"What's that for? I do not give you permission to use any pictures of me," Tazia barked.

"Then go back home. We don't need your sloppy journalistic writing up here. This is the big time." Claire spat. The two reporters were causing quite a scene when Dave, the night bartender, arrived for work. He grabbed Tazia by the arm and gently coaxed her into the kitchen.

"Your asshole friends can't hide you forever. Go home flat-lander!" Claire yelled in a catty tone.

"Claire, you need to leave the bar. Now!" Leslie glared down at the young reporter.

"There's a bigger story here, and I intend to expose it. You'll be sorry, you'll see," Claire fumed as she stormed out shoving her cell phone into her bag. Her high-heeled boots clomped across the wood floor sounding like a horse clopping on pavement.

A few minutes later Tazia came out of the kitchen and sat back down on the stool beside Leslie. "What was that all about?"

"I'm not sure," Leslie sighed. "But Chuck said he saw Claire and Titus Pritcher having drinks together a couple nights ago. Said he saw them leave together too."

"That could explain a lot." Tazia looked at Leslie's glass that was now empty. "What are you drinking?"

"A Hemingway Special, it's a drink my guys created. Similar to a Mojito. Want to try one?" Leslie picked up the empty glass and shook it a little.

"Later. I need to eat some dinner first."

"How about a break? You still like Italian, don't you?" Leslie slid off of her stool and picked up her purse.

"I like *an* Italian." Tazia chuckled, turned to Dave and waved. "I'll have one of those Hemingway Specials when I come back."

Dave nodded, smiled, and continued to work behind the bar, pouring drinks and putting dirty glasses in the sink. "It'll be waiting for you."

Leslie got them a booth beside a window in Rico's next door to the Casino. The space was colorful with walls painted green and red, framed posters of Italian landscapes and colorful villas hung on the walls, tables for four adorned with checkered tablecloths and candles, and soft Italian music playing in the background.

"Wait, what did you say? You like *an* Italian? Taz Drake, are you dating?" Leslie asked.

"What? Who said I was dating?" Tazia blushed, unable to hide her smile.

"It's about damn time. No offense. You know Chuck and I adored Simon, but you do need to move on with your life."

A young waitress with thick eyeliner, bright red lipstick, and wood brown hair in a ponytail that hung to the middle of her back handed them menus and glasses of water. "Would you like anything else to drink?"

"No, water's fine," Leslie said. "What about you Taz?"

"Water for me too."

"I'll be back in a minute to take your orders," the waitress smiled and strolled to another table of guests.

"Everyone's always telling me *I need to move on with my life*," Tazia said sipping her water. "I'm not up to full dating mode yet, but there is someone."

"Spill. I want all the details. An Italian in Whisper Creek?"

CHAPTER SEVEN

When they returned from dinner, Leslie and Tazia each got a Hemingway Special. They headed to one of the pool tables where Leslie racked the balls for a game. The bar was starting fill up and Dave and Gorbs were staying busy. Two other bartenders, Will and Smitty, had arrived to work as well.

They were not the typical bartenders, Tazia noticed as she occasionally glanced their way. The four guys laughed and seemed to party along with all the customers. They were just part of the crowd. No wonder they were so successful here.

She smiled and poised her pool cue for the nine ball in the corner pocket. As Tazia made the shot it felt like someone bumped her elbow and she completely missed the ball. She spun around to see who it was, but there was no one next to her. She rubbed her elbow and frowned at the confusion. She casually scanned the room that was filling up fast with people drinking and chatting. As she started to turn back to the pool table, something caught her eye.

A man at the bar with shoulder-length blond hair triggered an alarm in Tazia's mind. He strolled across the room and sat in a chair next to the *Authorized Personnel Only* door that led to the storage rooms and the upstairs. He turned and locked eyes with Tazia for a second. It was Victor, the man looking for work. Something scratched at the back of her neck as she looked over the man claiming to know the previous owners. She felt it again. Someone touching her elbow. But no one was there. It sent a chilling shiver through her whole body. A warning?

"I take it you didn't hire Vic?" Tazia asked, chalking the end of her pool cue.

"What?" Leslie looked over at the blond stranger leaning his chair against the wall. He had a backpack over the arm of his chair and a beer tilted up to his mouth. "No. I have plenty of staff." Leslie shot the eight-ball in and ended the game. "Come on; let me buy you another drink." They placed their cue sticks back in the rack and mingled with other customers as they made their way to the bar. Loud music and drunken laughter swayed through the large room.

Weaving her way through the customers, Tazia quickly claimed one of the two empty bar stools remaining. She turned to look over her shoulder at the blond out-of-towner. But he was gone. The backpack was gone. A half-empty glass of beer remained on the table. She looked through the crowd and at the doorway. No sign of him, but a strange feeling lingered in his absence. Tazia felt a hint of relief. She didn't have a problem helping people-in-need, but this man fell in a different category. One she couldn't quite put her finger on. She had a nagging sense that Victor wasn't what he claimed he was and suspected he was here for something very different.

Pushing thoughts of the stranger out of her mind, Tazia took another drink and smiled at Leslie. She was here to help her friend and have a good time. And damn it, that's what she was going to do.

Glasses and bottles clinked behind the bar, people laughed, the music played and balls knocked together on pool tables. Tazia could see why this was a good investment. *Sweet Caroline* played on the sound system and over half the people in the bar sang along with it. It was like hanging out with a large, drunk, and very happy family. Tazia felt a buzz on her cell phone and checked her text messages. Sure enough, there was one from Curtis, her boss. What did the old goat want now? She opened the message.

CURTIS: Back off on reporting any news from the Wood River Valley for now. Unless you have breaking news, quit stirring up trouble or come home.

She let out a heavy sigh and slid her phone back in her jacket pocket. "Dave, I'll have another one of those Hemingway drinks." She turned with her drink in hand and through the crowd Tazia noticed the *Authorized Personnel Only* door was ajar. Odd. Leslie had made a point the first day to keep that door shut.

An uneasy sensation tumbled through her body, like the electrical warning animals get before thunder.

The chill in her bones wasn't from the cold. "Storm's coming," Tazia whispered without even thinking.

CHAPTER EIGHT

Tuesday morning Tazia bundled up against the cold, stopped in at Starbucks for a tall chai latté, and headed back toward the Casino. She wanted to get an early start on some notes she was writing, even if she had been banned from writing an article for the paper. There was a story here, and she wanted to get it, one way or another.

She pulled her key out of her pocket to open the back door and noticed a homeless traveler curled up in a sleeping bag near the corner of the building at the edge of the alley. It made Tazia shiver.

"Hey, you want a hot cup of coffee?" she nudged his sleeping bag.

"Huh?" the old man pulled the bag over his head hiding from the morning air.

"Wait here," Tazia suggested, as if he were going anywhere. She entered the empty bar and pulled off her stocking cap. She quickly heated up a cup of coffee in the microwave, poured it in a Styrofoam cup and stepped back out into the alley and sat it on the ground next to the man sheltered from the cold. She placed a couple packs of sugar and creamers beside it on a napkin.

"What's your name?"

The old man with a face dark from age, whiskers and resentment, sat up and leaned against the wall. He reached out and picked up the coffee and took a sip. "Rex." He didn't look her in the eye but nodded a thanks for the coffee.

"See you around, Rex," Tazia stood up and headed back toward the door. Rex mumbled but said nothing more.

Inside, Tazia sipped her hot morning drink and took a look around the place. Nearly a hundred years of people imprinted their energy on the building. The quiet was layered with whispers of the past. Miners, gamblers, passers-through. She leaned against the end of the bar and reveled in the silence. It was an old building with a history of life, love, and death all of its own.

Readjusting her laptop bag's strap on her shoulder, Tazia walked across the old wood floor to the door marked *Authorized Personnel Only*. The storage room. The old poker room - the room a previous owner's wife lived in until her death not that long ago. And the stairway to the upstairs. The second floor hotel rooms and office. The third floor attic that was once a boarding room with rows of twin beds and chamber pots. And a ghost? Maybe even more than one spirit lingered in this building.

Dave had seen the spirit of a young girl around the age of ten. Over the years others had seen a woman upstairs. Second floor? Third floor? Leslie told her at least two men died on the second floor. Natural causes though. No foul play mentioned. But Tazia knew facts can get reshaped over time. She took another sip of the chai and reached for the doorknob. Time to get to work.

The office was at the front of the building on the second floor. Leslie and Chuck had completely redone it as well as the room across the hall. They were fairly modern with new sheetrock and paint on the walls, the old wood flooring buffed and smooth, and furnished for convenient use. Even a decent bathroom off the office. She shut the door though to keep the draft and the spirits from down the hall and upstairs away. She didn't want to think about them. She wanted to work.

A thump above her made Tazia stop and peer at the ceiling. She practically held her breath straining to listen to the strange sounds. Footsteps, fast. Fading then loud again as if running back and forth across the floor. But where? Who? She glanced at the door again to make sure it was shut tight. Then there were the sounds of creaking and cracking wood. Pounding. As if someone was pulling part of the wall out. She gulped.

Cautiously turning back to her computer, Tazia researched Titus's company, and scoured through past issues of the Mountain Messenger. It looked like a pretty good paper. But something about Claire really needled its way into her thoughts. Tazia's fingers hovered over her keyboard when a cat's meowing filtered through the room. She paused, tilting her head to listen. A knock on the door startled Tazia and she jumped, then turned around. The door opened and Leslie came in with a cup of coffee in hand.

"Hey, good morning," Leslie said and looked at her watch. "Or should I say afternoon? It's nearly twelve-thirty." She held up her coffee cup. "You want some?"

"Oh, it's you," Tazia let out a heavy sigh. "No thanks." She held up her Starbucks cup, stepped across the room and glanced out into the hallway. "Did you hear a cat just now?"

"There's no cats in here. Might be one outside on the roof." Leslie took a sip of her coffee. "I've been catching up on a little reading in the next room. Didn't want to disturb you too soon. Listen, I need to pull some things out of the attic for Saturday night and start getting that all set up. You wanna help?"

"Did you hear any other odd noises? Footsteps? Like from the attic?" Tazia looked to the ceiling again. "Is Chuck doing some work up there today?"

"No, he had to make a supply run. But, well, um, I mean…we hear odd sounds in this old building all the time. Maybe the boys are right, maybe there is a ghost up there. But I still need to get a couple of things from the attic. And I really don't want to go up there…alone."

"No problem," Tazia swallowed hard and closed her laptop. They started for the door when Tazia's cell phone rang. She pulled it out of her jacket pocket and glanced at the caller ID. She smiled. Matteo Alfieri. "I wanna take this, be with you in a minute." Tazia swiped to answer the call and turned her back to Leslie.

"Miss me yet?" Alfieri's sultry voice said on the other end of the line.

"Who are you again?" Tazia said, unable to hide the smile in her voice. She chuckled. "I'm keeping busy helpin' a friend. How 'bout you?" Tazia walked out into the hallway and headed toward the stairs that ascended to the attic. Leslie was already at the far end of the narrow hallway.

They chatted easily with noncommittal flirting in their words. "I've had a little run-in with the local reporter up here, who's watched too many movies or read too many detective novels. She seems to think I'm stealing some thunder from her by being here. Witchy little gal," Tazia said into the phone.

As Leslie disappeared around the corner and up the stairs to the attic, a scream filled the air with terror. "What was that?" Alfieri asked with his official cop voice. "Taz, what happened?"

"Either Leslie saw a ghost or a mutant spider. …" Tazia said running. When she reached the bottom landing of the stairs to the attic, she stopped and pulled her phone away from her ear.

"Call 9-1-1!" Leslie shrieked, backing up. The body of a man lay crookedly across the stairs. His head twisted, eyes still open looked into nothingness. His blond hair fell across his face. His arms and legs sprawled at odd angles. Tazia brought her phone back up to her ear.

"Gotta' go, I'll call you back later," she said.

"Wait! What's going on? What is it?" Alfieri demanded on the other end.

"Dead. He's dead. I'll call you back." Tazia ended the call and dialed 9-1-1. Leslie turned and wrapped her arms around Tazia. "Holy effen-shit!"

"Yes, we have a dead body," Tazia said with controlled calm into the phone. She was in shock, while Leslie was having a hysterical outbreak. Leslie took off down the hall and Tazia knelt down to look at the face. She tilted her head to match his gaze. It was Vic, the guy who wanted a job. *But what was he doing up here? What was he after? Hiding something? Looking for something? Meeting someone?*

The thought sent an icy prickle down Tazia's spine. Meeting someone up here? She stood looking up the staircase into the dark of the attic. Was someone still up there? She inched her way backwards off the bottom step that creaked under her foot. She put a hand out behind her to feel for the wall then turned and ran to the other end of the hall, down the stairs and into the bar.

Huffing from adrenaline and fear, Tazia stood wide-eyed in the bar. Two bartenders, Irish-looking Brent with his red hair and green eyes, and cute Will with his freckled boy-band round face, had rushed to the front door to find out what was going on. Leslie was coming in the entry way followed by paramedics and two local police officers. Will and Brent were close behind still asking questions.

"I'm Sergeant Todd, where's the body?" the uniformed officer asked. He was tall and bulky with a military haircut, solid square face and dark brown earthy eyes.

"Upstairs," Leslie pointed to the door Tazia had just come out of. "Third floor."

"Who found him?" Sergeant Todd asked.

"I…I did," Leslie's eyes glanced rapidly back and forth between the officer and the bar. She clearly wanted a drink.

"Do you know who he is?" Sergeant Todd asked as the first responder team headed up the stairs.

"His name is Vic, Victor, I think," Tazia gulped stepping beside Leslie. She and Leslie exchanged glances. "He came here looking for work a couple of days ago."

"That's right," Leslie said in a shaky voice. "He wanted a job. But I didn't have anything for him."

"When was the last time either of you saw him?"

Leslie shook her head with a blank look on her face and shrugged her narrow shoulders.

"I saw him last night, late, when the bar was full. He was sitting in a chair there against the wall." Tazia pointed.

Todd put his notebook back in his pocket and looked at the other officer, a scrawny red-headed young man. "Sykes, you go ahead and get everyone's statement down here." He looked around at the two bartenders and four patrons in the bar. "No one leaves until you get everything you need. Then let's shut the door until we know what we have." He glanced at Leslie, "Let's go have a look."

"If you don't mind, I'll have Tazia show you. I need a drink." Leslie didn't even wait for an answer, but turned on her heels and streamlined for the bar.

Sergeant Todd held the *Authorized Personnel Only* door open for Tazia to lead the way. She stopped for a moment. She didn't want to go back there either. She glanced over her shoulder to Leslie at the bar. This was the least she could do for her friend. She sucked in a deep breath, started up the stairs and looked back at the officer. "Well…what are you waiting for?"

They made their way up to the second floor hallway, down the narrow passageway and to the third floor landing. A man with a camera took pictures from all angles. He and a woman both had rubber gloves on, and they carefully sifted through the dead man's clothes. The woman pulled out a wallet and opened it up.

"Did he have anything else with him?" Officer Todd asked.

"No...oh, wait," Tazia replied. "He had a backpack. That was all I saw." Tazia retreated until her back was against the wall. She didn't want to get too close to Vic. His skin was discolored, and his dead eyes bothered her.

"Driver's license says Doug Ashburn, but the picture doesn't match," the female crime scene investigator said to no one in particular as she pulled the license out of the wallet. She slipped it and the wallet in an evidence bag and handed it to Todd. He put rubber gloves on and pulled the wallet out to look at the contents. Twenty dollars, a couple of credit cards, and the driver's license. "These are all Doug's."

"But, I mean... he said his name was Victor and he was friends with a Doug," Tazia said furrowing her brow.

"Why does he have Doug's..." Sergeant Todd said. He glanced at the woman with a sick expression. He pulled his cell phone out of his pocket.

"Charlie, yeah, this is Todd. I need you to reach the Ashburns, and see if you can reach their son Doug, too. Thanks." He slid the phone back into his pocket. He looked up at Tazia. "Do you know where the backpack is?"

"Sorry, no," she said, shaking her head. "Can I go now?"

"Sure, but wait downstairs. My partner will need to take your full statement."

"Will you do an autopsy? Do you know what killed him?" Tazia asked the examiners.

"At first glance, I'd say he fell down the stairs and broke his neck. But it's impossible to say for sure until we do the full exam. And yes, an autopsy has to be done when a death is questionable." They continued sifting through everything, then slipped a body bag around Vic. Tazia shuddered at the sound of them zipping up the heavy plastic as she retreated down the hallway. She glanced back before heading down and watched Sergeant Todd continue up to the attic, undoubtedly to look for the backpack. Normally she would be tagging along behind the officer. Hoping for a story after all, Tazia loved a good mystery as much as the next person. But the attic gave her the creeps.

When she got downstairs, Leslie was sitting on a stool at the end of the bar with a coffee cup in her hand.

"Want some?" Leslie asked.

"What's in it?"

"Just a little Baileys. I needed something to settle my nerves. I've never really seen a dead body before. I mean...dead. In the Casino."

"Sure," Tazia said to Will the bartender. "I'll have one of those too."

"Do you want a little coffee in your Baileys too?" Will asked. "So...a...dead body?" He said as he poured the Baileys into a coffee cup. He stopped for a moment and stared blankly at the *Authorized Personnel Only* door. Brent moved near Will and leaned onto the bar close to Leslie.

"Alex, I'll take who-dun-it for 600," he said.

"I'm sure...it was an...accident," Leslie stammered. "It had to be...right?" There was an edge of panic in her voice.

"Oh, grasshopper, you have much to learn," Tazia whispered beside her friend. Deep inside, Tazia wanted it to be an accident too. Simple and easy. But death, in her experience, was never simple and easy.

"It's barely after two o'clock in the afternoon," Leslie said in a daze, sipping her Baileys and coffee, staring at the *Authorized Personnel Only* door. "And I have a dead person upstairs."

"It's okay," Tazia said assuring her friend. "He'll be out shortly." They both sat sipping their coffees, staring at the door across the room.

It felt like an eternity before the door opened and Todd and the two crime scene employees emerged carrying the body. They'd left a gurney next to the door, which they placed Vic on and pushed it out the front of the building. Officer Sykes finished up his last round of questioning with an older gentleman at the end of the bar. He flipped his notepad closed, stuffed it in his pocket, and strolled over to meet up with Sergeant Todd.

"Well that's not going to be good for business," Leslie said arching her back then leaning forward to watch them leave the building. "Right out the front door in the middle of the day. What are people going to think?"

"If I know people, it'll just raise their curiosity," Tazia said. She looked over at Will. "You better get ready, I suspect you'll be super busy in here as soon as you reopen. Everyone'll be coming in to find out what happened."

"Huh," Leslie murmured with a grin inching across her thin lips. "I never thought of that." She pulled her cell phone out of her pocket. "I better call Chuck and let him know what's going on. He's going to freak!"

Officer Todd came back in and strolled up to Leslie and Tazia. "If you think of anything else, please give me a call. I'd like to get this investigation over and done with as soon as possible." He handed Leslie his business card.

"Will they tell us anything that they find? Like what happened? How he died?" Tazia asked in reporter mode. She turned to look at Leslie. "Do we know anything about him?"

"Just…" Leslie thought for a moment and shrugged. "That he was a college friend of Doug's from California, and he wanted a job. Said he'd do anything, bartend, wash dishes, do handyman shit. That was it. I didn't have any work and he was gone."

"Claimed he was a friend of Doug Ashburn, the previous owner's son, right?" The officer raised a questioning eyebrow.

"That's what he said," Leslie took another drink of coffee. "Said he was Doug's friend."

"Okay, we'll be following up on those leads. Ladies." Todd smiled and nodded his head before leaving. Leslie stared into an empty void, her eyes glazed over not focusing on anything. She drank the rest of her coffee and Baileys.

It was nearly five o'clock that evening when Leslie got the call from Sergeant Todd that she could open the Casino. But first floor only, he didn't want anyone going upstairs.

CHAPTER NINE

By seven o'clock guests and customers could barely squeeze in the doorway. It was just as Tazia had predicted. The word was out that someone was taken out of the Casino in a body bag, and everyone in town wanted first-hand news.

Who was it? What happened? Was it murder? The ghost? The rumor mill was charging ahead at full steam. Just about everyone in the Ketchum and Sun Valley area had stopped into the Casino bar. The numbers were unprecedented. Tazia clung to her barstool and watched in amazement. The death of a stranger didn't seem to damper anyone's mood though, and the drinking and laughter rose by the hour.

At half past seven that evening Tazia's Italian hunk edged his way into the bar. FBI Special Agent Matteo Alfieri, on indefinite loan from New York City to the Moon County Sheriff's Office, working with Tazia's uncle, Sheriff Madsen. Awkward to say the least. Awkward because she had sworn off romance and especially getting involved with law enforcement men. Awkward because here she was, falling for him and doing her best to deny it.

Tazia was a journalist, a Cubs fan, and a hell of a good poker player. He would never see in her face how she truly felt for him. At least, she hoped not. For in the back of her mind, she knew the attraction between them was dangerous. But she needed it. Something inside her even craved it. She'd already lost one man she loved to the line of duty, she couldn't bear to put herself in that position again. She'd sworn after Simon's death that she would never fall in love with a lawman a second time. She winced at the sight of Alfieri in the Casino. When their eyes met it sent a flutter from her chest clear to her abdomen.

"What's my favorite Tazmanian Devil doing this evening?" Alfieri asked squeezing between Tazia and the bearded man sitting on the stool beside her. The tight space in the crowded room demanded closeness, and Tazia shuddered as Alfieri's words pressed against her, his lips touching the edge of her ear.

"Drinking," Tazia held up her glass. "What are you doing here?"

"I heard a scream over the phone earlier, remember?"

"Oh that. So?"

Alfieri narrowed his eyes at her and crossed his arms over his chest. "What happened? You said you'd call me back." He looked at Gorbs behind the bar and caught his attention. He pointed to Tazia's glass. "Another round, please." He looked at Tazia's drink. "What is that, anyway?"

"It's a Hemingway Special, you should try it." She slid the nearly empty glass toward him. Alfieri took a sip.

"Make it two," Alfieri said to Gorbs. He pulled out his wallet.

"I'll run a tab for you," Gorbs said cheerfully and made the two drinks.

"Excuse me, excuse me!" A harsh voice pierced the crowd.

"Oh no," Tazia huffed. She looked over her shoulder to see Leslie ditching into the kitchen area. "Claire, you finally made it in, I see," Tazia yelled over the bar's noise.

"Where's Mrs. Brodie? I need to interview her right away. We have to get this murder story in our online feed tonight." Claire held out her phone with its recording app running.

Tazia tightened her jaw. Everything about funnel-girl Claire made Tazia cringe. The young eager reporter just rubbed her the wrong way. "Don't know." Tazia shrugged. "You should have come by earlier. This story's old news by now."

"Murder?" Alfieri raised an eyebrow, picked up his drink and took a sip.

"Covering what happens in the Casino isn't the only thing I have to do, you know. I have a life!" Claire huffed at Tazia with glaring eyes. "Who found him and who is he? What happened?"

"Yeah, Taz, who found him and who is he? What did happen?" Alfieri echoed the reporter. "Enquiring minds want to know." He flashed Tazia a steamy smile.

"Hey pal," Claire snarled at Alfieri, "This is *my* interview."

"Hey, I have the badge and the gun. Let's see yours," Alfieri said back to her, holding his jacket open to expose the Federal badge on his belt and the sidearm in his shoulder holster.

Claire's eyes got big as plates and she took in a deep breath, obviously assessing the situation. "This is a federal investigation?" her voice deepened.

"Oh no," Tazia sputtered through a laugh. "No, it's not a federal investigation. He's here as my friend, that's all. Don't blow this out of proportion." She punched Alfieri in the shoulder.

"How can I know I'm doing that if you won't tell me what's going on? I have a story to turn in. Where can I find the owners?" She frowned as she searched back and forth across the large room.

"Don't know. I'm just a customer having a drink," Tazia said. She picked up her glass and took a sip and smiled at Alfieri. "Cheers." She clinked her glass to his. Claire fumed, turned her recording app off and nudged her way up to the bar. She yelled over the conversations and the music for the bartenders to let her know where the owners were. But they weren't any more helpful than Tazia was. She finally drifted back into the crowd like a dolphin going out to sea.

"Okay, now the pest is gone, tell me what in the hell is going on here," Alfieri said expectantly. He rested a shoulder against hers.

"It wasn't murder; at least I don't think so. It looks more like an accident. It's hard to say." Tazia went on to fill Agent Alfieri in on all the details. He downed the rest of his drink and pulled out his cell phone. After scrolling through a few things, Alfieri looked up at Tazia. "Listen, I'm going to run down to the local LEOs and talk to them for a bit. It's best if I let them know I'm here. I'll see you back here after I'm done?"

"Sure," Tazia said after a moment of thinking about it. "I'll be around."

Tazia let out a heavy breath after Claire and Alfieri both left the bar. Glancing at her watch, she still had some time to work on her story. She wasn't sure where it would go, maybe just in a pile of unpublished ideas, but she wanted to write it. This building was hiding secrets, and she was a curious cat. She finished her drink and moved through the crowd to the other side of the room and the *Authorized Personnel Only* door.

When she reached the door, Tazia turned to see if anyone was watching her. They were all too busy talking, laughing and drinking. No sign of Leslie, so Tazia slipped through the door and up the stairs to the office on the second floor. Yellow crime scene tape was stretched across the far end of the hallway blocking the entrance to the attic. A wall of darkness stood beyond. That was fine with her. It was quieter upstairs, although the music found its way through the floorboards and joined with muffled sounds of overlapping conversations.

A light rain drizzled against the windowpane as Tazia opened her laptop. A cold chill ran down her back as a breeze seemed to sweep past her in the room as if someone had run by her. She turned abruptly, but no one was there. She got up and walked to the doorway and poked her head out into the hall. It was dark at the other end. The end where they had found Victor.

"Leslie?" Tazia said in a crackly voice. But her words dissipated into the shadows and no one answered. "Just an old drafty building," she whispered to herself and turned to go back to the desk by the window. "Hello there, and who are you?" Tazia said, smiling at a black cat with enormous green eyes who sat on the desk next to her laptop. "Where did you come from?"

The cat meowed as if to answer, then lightly jumped off the desk and walked past Tazia brushing against her leg. Tazia leaned over to pet the cat and see if she had a collar or name tag. Nothing. She'd never felt a cat so soft, it was as if her fur were cashmere. The cat looked into Tazia's eyes, meowed a low long utterance, then trotted down the hall to the far end, and up the stairs to the attic.

For a moment, Tazia wanted to follow the cat. She liked having the company. Still, there was a lingering question of where the cat had come from. She shook her head, closed the door and returned to her laptop hoping for no more surprises.

Thirty minutes later Tazia closed her research on the history of the Casino and saved some notes from the day's events, especially everything she could think of around the death of Victor. She stopped and stared at her computer screen for a moment thinking about the blond stranger. What was he doing up there? Had he been looking for something? Was he hiding something? Meeting someone?

The stairs creaked out in the hall and Tazia knew someone was coming up. But then she knew she was never alone in the old building. She closed her laptop and turned to get up. The door opened slowly and Leslie poked her head in the room.

"Is it clear yet?" Leslie asked.

"You scared me there for a minute. Don't creep up on me like that!" Tazia held her hand to her chest.

"Sorry, I needed to get away from the craziness around that guy, Victor. I don't want that getting into the press with our grand opening so close. But…" Leslie blew out a heavy breath and looked around the room, then stared out the window past Tazia. "I suppose there's no getting around it." She looked back at Tazia as she slumped into a chair beside the desk. "How can I minimize the damage though? I mean, I'm horrified that someone died here, and I feel bad for him and his family, but still…" she said with a furrowed brow and ran her hand through her thin shoulder length hair. "I also don't want this getting blown out of proportion."

"Murder getting blown out of proportion?" Tazia laughed then leaned forward with her elbows on her knees and rested her chin on her fists. "I think the point we want to make clear is that this was an accident. That's step one. No matter what the police say, we need to stand our ground as long as we can, at least until after Saturday. That may even bring more people in for the grand opening. I mean…" Tazia waved a hand in a sweeping motion. "Look at the crowds today. Everyone wants to know what happened. If we can keep that curious buzz going, you should be fine. How's Chuck doing?"

"Chuck's a rock. I'd be tightening the straps on my white jacket if it weren't for him. Hey, he thinks we should create a special drink for the grand opening. What do you think of that? We could start advertising it today on our social media and get all the bartenders to start mentioning it."

Standing up and brushing her pant legs down, Tazia smiled at her friend. "I think you guys have something there, Les. Seriously. I'll start posting on my social medias too about the buzz around the new drink your bartenders are creating. In fact, call the drink the *Big Reveal.* I like it." Tazia strolled across the room and looked past Leslie down the hall to the far end. "I just saw the cat again. She must have found a way in."

"A cat?" Leslie followed Tazia into the hallway. "I've never seen a cat in here. Are you sure?"

"There was one in here just a bit ago. A big black cat with intense green eyes. She was beautiful, then she walked down the hall and up into the attic." Tazia nodded in that direction with her chin. "You've never seen her?"

"And what were you drinking before you came up here?" Leslie chuckled and shook her head. "Don't you get weird on me too. I have enough of that from the crowds downstairs." Leslie put her arm around Tazia's shoulder. "Come on, what are you doing for dinner?"

"Oh, Alfieri," Tazia said suddenly remembering. "Uh...the guy I told you about. He's...um..."

"Spit it out girlfriend, what's got your tummy in a knot?"

"Matteo Alfieri," Tazia mumbled. Just to speak his name sent a flutter through her insides. The images and feelings the thought of him produced caused havoc with her senses. His kiss. His touch. She swallowed. "Alfieri's up here. Anyway, I think he's planning to take me to dinner." She felt her face flush simply talking about it.

They started down the stairs. "Oh really?" Leslie said. "I can't wait to meet this special agent of yours."

When they entered the first floor, Tazia saw Alfieri leaning against the bar with a drink in one hand. She smiled and wove through the crowd to reach him with Leslie on her heels.

"Matteo Alfieri, my friend and owner of the bar, Leslie Brodie," Tazia said as she stood between the two.

"Well, my husband and I own the bar, but he's rarely in here when there's a crowd. He handles all the remodel work, I handle the business of the bar." Leslie held out her hand to Alfieri.

"Delighted to meet you," Alfieri said through a polite smile as he shook her hand. "Mind if I steal this lady away for dinner?" He finished his drink and set the empty glass on the bar without taking his steel grey eyes off of Tazia.

"Be my guest. You two kids have fun," Leslie laughed and made her way into the kitchen area behind the bar.

Outside, the storm had passed but left the night air thick and wet. They walked down the sidewalk together to the restaurant on the corner of the block.

"How's Grandmother?" Alfieri asked, wrapping an arm around Tazia's shoulder.

"*My* grandmother is just fine," she said, glaring up at him. They both chuckled. Alfieri, ever the gentleman, opened the door and held it for Tazia to walk in. He checked in with the front counter, apparently he'd made a reservation. They were shown to a small table near the back of the room beside a window. The soft lights of the elegant restaurant were inviting and even romantic. Candle centerpieces flickered on each table. The aromas of rich meat sizzled on a nearby grill and heavy sauces wafted through the room. Alfieri moved behind Tazia and began to pull her coat off, then stopped and lowered his lips to her neck. The heat of his breath made her heart race. He stepped back and pulled a chair out for her to sit.

"What's with the service? I suppose you open and close a lady's car door too?" Tazia sat and watched as he pulled his own coat off and sat across from her.

"Damn right." He smiled. "Chivalry's not dead, just dormant." Picking up the menu, he looked at Tazia. "Want a cocktail or a glass of wine with dinner?"

"Wine would be nice. I prefer red wines."

"How about a good Malbec? Better with steak," Alfieri replied glancing down at the menu. Ceiling fans whirred, patron's cutlery clinked, and conversations were low and private. After giving the waitress their order and receiving their glasses of wine, Alfieri rolled his shoulders and looked at Tazia as if he had something to say, but wasn't sure how to say it.

"What?" Tazia asked.

"That guy, Victor," he leaned toward her.

"Yeah, what about him?"

"His name's Victor Nellis, but he also had Doug Ashburn's wallet and ID in his pocket."

"That doesn't sound good."

"No. They're tracking Doug and his family down now. Apparently Doug's parents were the previous owners of the Casino." Alfieri twirled his wine glass then took a sip.

"Why was Victor here?" Tazia wondered.

"The Ketchum police are working on it."

"He did say he was a friend of Doug's. From college, I think," Tazia persisted.

Alfieri smiled, obviously trying to decide how much information to share. "All I can say…is the local police are trying to find Doug now for questioning." He picked up his wine again and took a sip.

"So I get the feeling something's wrong with this picture, though. Right?" Tazia looked over her wine glass into his winter grey eyes.

"Correct. There must be something Doug told him about the Casino that brought him here. Do you have any ideas what that might be?"

"There's nothing …oh wait." Tazia rolled her eyes. "There's stories, old stories, that Doug's father, or grandfather buried money or treasure in the walls of the upstairs. Leslie said someone's already torn boards and plaster off looking for it. But nothing was ever found. Not even decent insulation."

"That doesn't stop someone like Victor from believing that it's still there." Alfieri took another sip of wine. "The local police chief is going to start looking all around the attic and the second floor of the Casino tomorrow morning. He's agreed to let me tag along."

Tazia perked up. "Can I tag along too?"

He tilted his chin and gave her a you-know-better-than-that look. "Until stated otherwise, that's an active crime scene. There's too many unanswered questions at this point. First we need to find out if anyone else was up there with him."

"I think there was," Tazia murmured.

"Who?"

"The cat." She smiled and leaned back as the waitress set their steak dinners down in front of them. "And the ghost."

Agent Alfieri raised an eyebrow in amusement. "Of course," he chuckled.

CHAPTER TEN

After finishing a superb New York cut of steak, medium rare, a baked potato loaded and a warm roll smothered in honey butter, Tazia was ready to get back to the Casino. She listened intently to the conversations around the restaurant as Alfieri paid the check for their dinner and drinks. Murmurs and whispers of "the Casino" and "found dead" floated on aromas of steak and crab dinners as they passed to tables of newly arrived customers. She didn't feel comfortable discussing too much of the case in this place. Too many ears that seemed to be listening. At least at the Casino, the music played loud enough you didn't hear conversations except your own.

The wet pavement from the earlier rainstorm reflected the street lights. Tazia shoved her hands deep in her jacket pockets. "I'm not writing anything on this for the paper, you know. I'm just worried for my friends. I don't want this to turn ugly for their new business."

"I get it. But there's nothing to tell anyone right now. All we've got is Victor in the morgue and a questionable incident." Alfieri wrapped his strong arm around her shoulder and pulled her close.

"But you will let me know when it gets ruled crime or accident?" Tazia looked up into his eyes and gazed sensually at his lips.

"Yes," Alfieri smiled down at her. "I'll let you know what I can. Just be patient."

"Hmph" Tazia rolled her eyes. Patience wasn't something she was good at, and she didn't care. Patient reporters didn't get the story first. She had no desire to be patient.

Tazia glanced up at Alfieri after they entered the Casino. "Care for a game of pool?" she asked.

"I hate to make you feel bad by losing to me all night," Alfieri said as they made their way to the bar. "Two Hemingway Specials," he called to Dave behind the bar.

"You mean you don't want to be shown up by a female. Isn't that more like it? You don't want to lose to *me* all night." Tazia leaned against the bar tilting her head up to him. "Don't worry, the night might not be a total loss." She picked up the drink and took a sip, looked over at Dave. "Thanks Dave, these are fantastic!"

Alfieri dodged the crowd making his way to one of the three pool tables in the back of the bar. All three were taken at the moment, so he sat on an empty stool near the wall and watched the players.

Table one was two guys, a short man with no visible hair under a baseball cap, and a taller guy with long hair pulled back in a ponytail. The tall man was a regular who came in every evening with his own cue stick, played a few games of pool, drank a couple of beers then left. He didn't stay long. He was always in and out in under two hours. He was friendly and cheerful, and he always flashed Tazia a genuinely friendly smile when he passed her. Dave had told her the guy rarely missed a night. He would come in after work, play his games, drink his two beers, then be on his way. There was cool precision about every move he made, from entering the bar to making his shots. She liked watching him. He was calculated and accurate. He knew what he was doing.

When the two guys were done, the tall one nodded to Tazia. "It's all yours, babe," he said as he pulled his custom cue stick apart and slid it into its carrying case. "Have a good one." He winked at her as he walked by. Alfieri gave him a suspicious look with squinted eyes.

"Who's that guy? You know him?" Alfieri asked as he racked the balls on the table preparing for a new game.

"Local Bob? No, just see him come in every night to play his pool then leave. He never stays long, but he's consistent."

"You don't like unpredictable? Spontaneity?" Alfieri whispered in her ear as he passed by her reaching for a cue stick from the selection on the wall. "What *do* you like in a guy?" He leaned over the edge of the table to take the breaking shot. A wry grin on his mouth.

"Are you taking notes?" Tazia smirked. She leaned against the edge of the table, stroked the cue stick in her hand and licked her lips flashing him a sultry smile.

Alfieri missed his shot.

CHAPTER ELEVEN

The early morning clouds were breaking up with patches of blue sky and the warm sun peeking through. It was a welcome change. Tazia had gone for an early morning jog and arrived at the front door of the Casino at the same time Dave the bartender did. They were greeted by a large broad chested man and a middle-aged woman with unnaturally bright red hair, sheer black nylons and spiked high heels. The couple seemed agitated and impatient as they fidgeted on the sidewalk. The man looked at his watch and shot a glare to the red head.

"Can I help you?" Dave asked as he got his key out to open the front door. "We're not open yet."

"I'm Donna Sanchez," the woman said in a nasally voice. "This is Titus Pritcher from California," she added in an irritated impatient way. Tazia crinkled up her nose at the strong perfume the woman wore that smelled like a flower shop had exploded, and not in a good way.

"And I'm Dave from Ketchum, Idaho. The bar opens in an hour."

"And I'm Tazia Drake from Whisper Creek, Idaho," Tazia chimed in.

"I don't think you understand," huffed the large, broad-chested man. "I'm Titus Pritcher, I'm buying this whole block."

"Well, technically, this end of the block." The red head corrected him. "All the buildings on this side of the block." She waved her hand from the small real estate office on the left side of the Casino bar, past the bar, the barber shop to the corner with the Italian restaurant on the right. "We'll be making an offer today."

"I didn't know it was for sale," Tazia mused.

"Everything's for sale for the right price," Titus Pritcher smirked, his curved lips baring teeth.

"Well folks, like I said," Dave unlocked the door. "The place will open in an hour. See you then."

The shapely red head and Titus looked at each other, then narrowed their eyes on Dave and Tazia. "We'll be back," the red head snapped, whipped out her business card and shoved it at Dave. He glanced at it. Donna Sanchez, Mountain Realty.

"Whatever," Dave mumbled and stuffed the card in his pocket.

Donna Sanchez looked at her Apple watch and then up at her client Titus. "One hour," she said.

"There's a Starbucks around the corner." And off they went like a thundering elephant and a jittery ostrich.

"That bitch," Dave said as he hung his coat up and started sorting through things behind the bar. "You want some coffee?"

"Sounds great. So who is she? That real estate agent." Tazia asked as she scooted onto a bar stool. She pulled a pen and notepad out of her pocket and jotted down some ideas. "Chuck and Leslie just bought this place, I mean, their grand re-opening is in two days. Why on earth would they sell it now?"

"They wouldn't," Dave said coming out of the kitchen. "Coffee will be ready in a couple of minutes. "They're just blowing smoke, trying to get a rise."

"Not everything's about the money." Tazia poised her pen over the small note pad.

"It's not about the money. Not with this place. The Casino's on the historic register. This place, these people – mean something to this town. Look at me," Dave said leaning against the back bar, crossing his arms over his chest. "I've been bartending here for thirty years. Do you think that happens at most bars? Hell no. But this place isn't just a bar. It's a warm gathering place for locals and friends. Sure the tourists come in here, who wouldn't?" Dave chuckled. He peeked around the corner into the kitchen area and walked over to the coffee pot. He called out from the other room. "Black, right?"

"Yes," Tazia called back. She scribbled some notes on her pad.

"You see," Dave continued as he set the cup of black coffee in front of Tazia and leaned back again sipping his own coffee. "These out-of-state developers think they can waltz in here and take over. But they have no idea who they're dealing with in this place." He winked and took another sip.

"Morning guys," Leslie and Chuck walked in from the kitchen. "I have a few things to finish up today, before Saturday's big event. But everything's falling into place. I just want to double check the inventory today," Leslie said.

"Mornin' boss," Dave nodded at Leslie then Chuck. "Coffee's ready."

"What would I do without you," Leslie kissed Dave on the cheek and headed back into the kitchen area.

"I'll be doing a final check of everything in the restrooms, the kitchen, and the café today. What about behind the bar? Anything I need to check there?" Chuck asked.

"Na," Dave said. "Everything's running smooth here. But I noticed the icemaker was having a few hiccups last night," Dave stepped around the corner to the large commercial icemaker and Chuck followed him. He turned and looked over his shoulder at Leslie. "Oh hey, some Tight-ass Prick guy stopped by, said he'd be back when we open."

"*Titus Pritcher*," Tazia enunciated more clearly. "He claims he's making an offer." She raised a questioning eyebrow.

"An offer on what?" Chuck asked as he came back out and stood next to his wife.

"Here," Dave grabbed the business card out of his pocket and held it out to Chuck. "On the whole property. The idiot thinks he can get the place." Dave set a rack of clean glasses on the back counter and started putting them away on the shelves behind the bar. "Typical out-of-town developer."

"Yes, Tight-ass made an offer when it first went on the market." Leslie snickered. "But he wanted to tear all this down. The office space next door, the Casino, the barber shop and even the restaurant on the corner and build all new. The locals are dead set against it. And the previous owners said no way. They wanted the building to stay intact."

"I don't blame them. We're losing too much of our history in this state as it is," Dave said.

"So when Chuck and I offered to buy it, agreeing to keep it as it is with only minimal renovations, *and* to keep all the current staff, we got the deciding vote."

Tazia smiled. "I'm glad. You guys are all so awesome. And while all the other bars across the street are new and fancy, this one has real character."

She set her coffee cup down and looked up gazing over the old timbers that gave the building life. "You can't build that from something new."

Leslie stepped into the small kitchen area and topped off her coffee, then came back out and leaned against the end of the bar looking at Tazia. "Where's your hubba hubba fella' today?" she asked.

"Alfieri? He's not..." Tazia rolled her eyes. She wanted to say he was nothing more than a friend, a coworker of sorts. But she didn't like to lie. "He's staying at a hotel in Hailey. He was going to be at the police station today, said he'd check in with me later." Tazia sipped her coffee.

"Chuck and Leslie Brodie?" the red head real estate agent said as she and Titus Pritcher marched into the bar.

"Speaking of..." Dave chuckled and went back to putting away the glasses.

"Can we see the upstairs?" Donna Sanchez asked holding a hand out to the *Authorized Personnel Only* door across the room. "I heard you had a man die up there yesterday. Murder? That can't be good for business." Her words rolled across her tongue like slime off a slug. It made Tazia gag just a bit.

Chuck stepped forward with Leslie right on his heels. The cocky developer was twice Chuck's size in height and width, but Chuck stood his ground like a protective bulldog. "Titus, you already know this place isn't for sale. And even if it was, the city would never let you do what you want. This building's on the historic register." Chuck folded his arms across his chest and glared at the large man in front of him.

"No one was murdered here. You better watch that forked tongue of yours, Donna," Leslie spat at the red head. "Nasty rumor spreading can come back and bite you in the ass." Donna and Leslie exchanged hostile stares.

Chuck pulled his wife back a step and spoke to Titus. "Listen, the place isn't for sale. If you want a drink, then Dave can set you up. Otherwise, we're done here."

"Oh we're not done, not by a long shot," Titus's voice boomed across the empty room. "I'm buying this place. You'll see." He twisted his large body around and elbowed Donna, then nodded at her to follow him out. The elephant man and the ostrich lady stormed out of the bar.

"Do you think he had anything to do with Victor's death? I mean," Leslie looked at Tazia. "What if he did that to create bad press for the place? What if he's really that desperate to get it? Just think what else he'd do!" Leslie's voice was rising in pitch with each word. Chuck pulled her around to face him and held his hands on her shoulders. "Hon, he didn't have anything to do with that guy upstairs. He's just trying to rattle you. He's nothing but a big bag of hot air."

But it was clear to Tazia that Leslie was unnerved by the whole visit. It was a valid question. How far would Titus Pritcher go to get his hands on this property?

CHAPTER TWELVE

Shortly after noon on Friday, Tazia noticed her friend Leslie was so stressed she looked like she'd stuck a finger in a light socket. Her curls were untamed and her eyes were glazed over. Tazia kept trying to calm her down, assure her that Titus was bluffing on everything, but her friend was too high up the panic ladder.

"I have to get the inventory done," Leslie said shaking her head and running her trembling hands through her frizzled hair.

"Go do what you need to do, I've got this out here," Dave said from behind the bar. Leslie strode over to the storage room mumbling to herself.

The front door of the bar swung open and someone rushed into the room. Tazia spun around to see what was going on and found herself face to face with funnel-girl Claire, the reporter.

"You can't fool me," Claire sputtered into Tazia's face. "I know you're up here to cover a story. But I beat you to it! So go home flat-lander." Claire threw a newspaper on the counter of the bar, smirked and stomped out of the place.

"What in the hell is she babbling about?" Dave asked as he picked up the local newspaper and flipped through the pages. He stopped suddenly, his mouth agape and the color drained from his face. "Ho-ly shit! Leslie's going to explode when she sees this!"

"What?" Tazia grabbed the paper out of his hands and read it. "New owners of the Casino bar stage fake events to draw in customers for grand re-opening." Her eyes got bigger with disbelief as she read on. "No one was murdered and the building isn't haunted by ghosts old or new." Tazia looked up at Dave with puzzlement on her face. "What the hell *is* she talking about? How do they get away with printing this shit?"

"From what I know, the publisher is out of town for a month, Europe or something, and you know what they say, 'when the cat's away'…" Dave shook his head and rolled his eyes.

"The mice hang themselves," Tazia said. "And she's got her byline and photo next to the article. She wants everyone to know *she* wrote this. *She's* the one who got the story. Too bad they don't know she writes fiction." Tazia threw the paper on the bar, crossed her arms over her chest and huffed. She rolled some ideas around in her head for a minute, then ran upstairs taking two steps at a time to sit down at her laptop and control her breathing and her emotions. *Calm down. Not every journalist is ethical.*

You can't control them, only yourself. She closed her eyes and pulled in deep breaths letting them out slowly. *After all, she thought, someone has to write for the Enquirer. I should send them Claire's resume.*

Opening her laptop and logging in, Tazia spent the first few minutes browsing the home page of her paper, the Herald. She needed to see if anything was happening back home that she was missing. Nothing out of the ordinary. It was a quiet week in Moon County. It certainly wasn't quiet up here. She spent the next hour researching Claire the reporter. Fresh out of college. Figures. Wanting to make a name for herself but not knowing the right way to do it.

Egos.

Mid-afternoon Leslie stepped into the upstairs office, paced the room for a couple of minutes then plopped down in a chair beside Tazia.

"This is cracked. We have a dead person in the morgue that no one knows much about. We have a bat-shit-crazy young reporter printing lies. We have an idiot developer and his mistress of the looney bin trying to bully us into selling. And to top all that off, we have our grand opening tomorrow night. *Tomorrow!*" Leslie's voice was shrill with panic. "And I'm losing my mind," she mumbled shaking her head, pulling out her cigarette pack. "I can't go into the attic, it's still taped off." She flicked her lighter and took a drag off the cigarette. "We sunk a lot of money into the advertising for this event, and stocking everything for it. I mean," Leslie let out a puff of smoke. "I never dreamt anything like this would happen."

"No one would," Tazia leaned forward with her elbows on her knees, chin resting in her palms. "It's crazy, but sometimes crazy just happens and you deal with it. Your grand opening is going to be even better than you thought. Claire's article isn't going to stop anyone. The locals know her and they know you. But most of all, they know this place. They love the Casino, it's theirs."

"I hope you're right," Leslie leaned her head back looking up to the ceiling. She took a long slow drag off her cigarette. "I hope you're right."

The ring of Leslie's cell phone startled her and she jumped, dropped her cigarette and dove to pick it up. She jerked the phone out of her jacket pocket and answered. "The Casino, Leslie...yes, but she left hours ago. Of course." Leslie ended the call and slipped the cell phone back in her pocket looking at Tazia with a furrowed brow. "Have you heard from Claire since she left here?"

"Funnel-girl?"

"Funnel-girl?" Leslie asked with a raised eyebrow.

"Oh, sorry, I mean Claire. No, I haven't. Why?"

"That was someone from the paper. Apparently, Claire was supposed to be there for an important meeting or something, and she never showed up. They're tracing her steps, I guess." Leslie shrugged and took another drag off her cigarette.

"She's not answering her phone? Somehow that doesn't sound like her. Even from what little I know. Reporters don't blow off meetings and ignore phone calls. Staying connected is our life blood."

"Exactly," Leslie said. "What's wrong? You look a little pale all of a sudden."

"It's just...a feeling. I'm sure it's nothing. I think I'll go for a walk, get some fresh air. I've been in here all day." Tazia closed her laptop, stood up and brushed down her pant legs. She'd always had a sixth sense, especially when it came to warnings of danger. And her sixth sense was screaming in her ear that something was terribly wrong. "I'll be back in a little while to help with anything, if you need."

"No, don't worry about it. I have everything under...oh who the hell am I kidding? I don't have anything under control. But Dave and Brent and the other bartenders, they do. They're the ones that really run this place. The Casino's nothing without them." Leslie let out a puff of smoke on a heavy sigh.

"Don't underestimate yourself so much. They may be the blood that runs through the veins of this place, but you're the heart that keeps them pumping."

Tazia gave her friend a hug and skipped down the stairs.

Stepping out onto the sidewalk of Main Street, Tazia pulled her cell phone out of her coat pocket and hit the speed dial icon for Matteo Alfieri. Few people understood Tazia's psychic connection to other things. She didn't completely understand it herself. But she'd learned to trust it. And the voices of her ancestors, as her Grandmother called them, were coming through loud and clear. Danger was in the air. "Alfieri, have time for a quick meeting?" She picked up her pace and turned left heading to a great sandwich shop she'd found. Alfieri was waiting on the cafe's patio for her by the time she got there.

"What's up? You sound a little worried," Alfieri said as he held the door open for her. They ordered coffee and pastries and sat in a booth by a window. "While I'm delighted to hear from you, somehow I don't feel like this is just your desire to see my handsome face," Alfieri said in his deep, sexy voice. He winked at her, smiled and took a sip of coffee.

"You know how I get...feelings. I..." Tazia didn't know how to put into words the vision that pressed against her mind. "Claire. It's that reporter from the local paper. Someone from her work called looking for her. She missed a meeting, I guess, and isn't answering her phone."

"So? You don't even like the girl," Alfieri pinched off a corner of an apple turnover and nibbled on it.

"It's not about whether I like her or not." Tazia felt flustered. It was hard to explain her visions to other people. "I hope I'm wrong, but I feel like she's in danger."

"What exactly are you sensing?" Alfieri's tone changed. He acknowledged her intuition, swallowed the last bite of his pastry and picked up his coffee cup, the steam drifting up to his chin.

"A dark shadow around her. And someone who is just out of sight, but he has her. And it's not good," Tazia held both hands tight around her coffee cup. "When I try to see it more clearly, I feel like I'm suffocating."

"The Shadow Man?" Alfieri whispered. She noticed a flash in his eyes.

"The who?"

"No one, just thinking out loud. Do you see anything else? Any little detail at all?" There was urgency in Alfieri's voice. This obviously struck a chord. His grey eyes had gone from carefree to serious, even frantic.

"No," Tazia said softly trying to remember. She closed her eyes for a moment to pull the vision in as tightly as possible. "It's like a tall man, completely shrouded in black, I can't see any physical details. Nothing. But he's holding her with an...intention..."

"What?" Alfieri pushed.

"An intention to," Tazia murmured.

"I know what his intention is. I have to go," Alfieri said as he took a drink of his coffee and stood up. "You're going back to the Casino and staying close to your friends there. You hear me?" There was deep worry in his eyes that echoed on his voice. "Don't go off on your own, don't agree to meet anyone you don't know. Stay with your friends. I'll see you there later tonight."

"But where are you going?" Confused, Tazia stood up in front of him. "Let me come," she reached out and touched his arm.

"No, not this time," Alfieri's voice was sincere but firm. He put his hands on her shoulders and kissed her forehead. "Promise me you'll stay with your friends. I'll see you tonight at the Casino." He reached into his pocket and pulled out his wallet. He dropped a five-dollar bill on the table and put a hand on the small of Tazia's back nudging her to the door. "Come on, I'll walk you back to the bar and then you're going to stay there."

"Not even Grandmother gets away with telling me what to do," Tazia smirked as they strolled to the door. She stopped once they got outside and looked up at him. "But something tells me you're right. I don't know how or why, but I'll stay with Leslie and Chuck." Her first instinct was to go with him. He had a lead, she could feel it. And she didn't want to miss out on anything. But the sense of impending danger that hung over her swayed her, and she agreed to do as he asked. This time.

They walked with their heads bent blocking a northern wind that swept through the small mountain town.

"By the way," Alfieri said as they walked. "We found something on Victor Nellis. He has a warrant out for his arrest for several robbery and drug charges." Standing outside of the Casino, Alfieri put a hand under Tazia's chin and gently pulled it up to meet his face. He kissed her on the lips, warm and caring. He pulled back a step to look at her more carefully and brushed some hair out of her face. She loved his touch. It reverberated through her entire body warmer than a shot of whiskey on a cold day. He waited while she walked into the Casino. Tazia turned once she was inside to wave goodbye, but he was already gone.

Finding it hard to be still, Tazia paced the bar waiting for news from Alfieri. She pulled out her cell phone and searched the number for the local newspaper. "Hi," she said into the phone as she stood in a quiet corner of the bar. "I'm looking for your reporter Claire. Is she there?" But Tazia knew before they answered that she wasn't. Still, she hoped she was wrong. "No, no, thanks. I'll try later." She disconnected the call and put the phone back in her pocket. "Drama queens," she mumbled to herself. She hoped this wasn't something intentional on Claire's behalf to get attention. Another headline. But as she strolled over to the bar, she knew it wasn't Claire's doing. Whatever was happening, this was on someone else.

The shadow man. The thought penetrated her mind, something she'd heard Alfieri mention in the past. Wasn't he the serial killer Alfieri'd been chasing? Did he think the shadow man was in Ketchum?

"I'm ready for a beer," Tazia leaned against the bar smiling at Will who was putting away clean glasses. "Miller Lite."

"One Miller Lite coming right up," Will was the youngest bartender at thirty-two, who loved sharing stories of his side job as a snow board instructor. He jiggled his round body, dancing to the music as he poured drinks and told jokes to anyone who would listen. Tazia scooted onto the leather covered bar stool and sipped her beer.

"Hey, Will, what do you think makes this bar so popular?" Tazia asked.

"That's right," Will threw a dish towel over his shoulder and did a shimmy then laughed. "You're the writer friend of Leslie's. Well, I gotta' say there's no other place for miles quite like this." He nodded to the barber shop entrance at the end of the bar. "They come in here to get a haircut, have a cocktail, play a game of pool, and laugh at my jokes. What's better than that?" Tazia tilted her beer at him in a toast, then took a long drink.

The bar was starting to fill up, guys playing pool, people sitting at the tables and the bar drinking, laughing, talking. A Jimmy Buffet song danced through the air. Tazia tried to relax as much as possible, but she still couldn't shake the sense of impending danger. And for whatever reason, it kept feeling like it was getting closer. She didn't always understand her visions; these things her Grandmother said were voices of their ancestors. Tazia took another drink of beer wishing her ancestors would shut up.

CHAPTER THIRTEEN

Tazia leaned back against the bar and faced the room. She was on her second beer as she observed the crowd, and listened for clues she could use. Bits and pieces of information that might drift in and out of conversations around her. Murmurs about Victor and his death. A whisper about Claire. It was half past seven in the evening, and still no word of the annoying reporter. Tazia's sense of impending danger for the girl hadn't gone away. In fact, it had intensified.

"Leslie, there you are," Tazia chirped as her friend came into the bar from the kitchen. "The crowd seems self-involved with no interest in earlier events."

"Life is good." Leslie nodded at Will behind the bar. "I'll have a margarita on the rocks." She turned back to Tazia. "I've been pulling my hair out getting ready for tomorrow. Look," Leslie grabbed a handful of thin curly hair holding it up. "Almost none left!"

"Hey, I could really use some fresh air. Go for a walk with me? Just to the corner and back?" Tazia asked.

"Sure, it might do me some good too." Leslie took a slug of the margarita and set it behind the bar. "I'll finish this when we get back." She wrapped her arm through Tazia's folded arm and they headed out the front door.

Outside the moon hid behind thick clouds and the cold pressed against their faces. They both shivered and stepped closer to each other for warmth.

"I need to grab something in the cabin, let's go round back." Leslie nodded to the left. They walked around the block and into the alley. A scuffling sound echoed through the night and then the crash of a knocked-over can startled the two women.

"Who's there?" Leslie called out.

Tazia pulled her cell phone out and hit the flashlight app shining it on the edge of the building. A man in layers of dark heavy clothes stood up. He looked like a homeless man with a dirty rolled up sleeping bag next to him.

"It's just me, Rex. Sorry ma'am. I was just staying out of the cold. Heavy wind tonight." He stood and edged away from the building into the alley. "I'll be on my way." He dropped his head to his chest and loped down the alley to the other end.

"This valley isn't the best to be homeless in. The winters are too damn cold," Leslie huffed as she took her keys out of her jacket pocket and opened the cabin door. "Come on, I just need to grab some papers and a new pack of smokes." Leslie grabbed a couple of folded papers off the small kitchen table and dug in a drawer for a pack of cigarettes. She stuffed both in her jacket pocket and looked at Tazia. "I still can't figure out this Vic guy. Did he think we had drugs hidden in the walls?"

"No, I'm sure he was hoping to find money, or something of value he could pawn," Tazia sat down on the sofa in the cozy living room.

"Ah yes, the old rumors," Leslie slumped into the chair on the other side of the wood stove and opened the pack of cigarettes she'd just stuffed in her pocket. Her hands shook as she flicked her lighter and inhaled the nicotine. "I'm so rattled from everything. The asshole developer, the opening tomorrow, the guy dying upstairs, and that article in the newspaper. I mean, how am I supposed to deal with all of this?" She took a long drag off her cigarette and slowly let the smoke escape from her mouth and curl up around her lip.

"Oh, I haven't had a chance to tell you." Tazia leaned over the arm of the couch. "Alfieri has been working with the local police, anyway, this Doug guy is missing. No one's seen him in a week." Tazia wrapped her arms around herself. "I suspect foul play and I'll bet this Vic's involved."

"Doug?"

"Yeah, remember? Vic had Doug's wallet on him. He said Doug's parents used to own the Casino, and recommended Vic come here to get a job."

"Doug Ashburn. Damn!" Leslie let her hands fall down over the arms of the chair and her eyes grew big. "Do you think this Vic guy's a murderer?"

"Hard to say," Tazia said. "We don't know what happened in California. But the police have scoured the entire attic and the second floor. They've cleared your building and all you have to focus on is your grand opening tomorrow. The developer, the real estate agent and even the news article are out of your hands. Forget them."

"You're right," Leslie took another drag off her cigarette. "I have a tendency to get ahead of myself. To overthink things."

"You think?" Tazia laughed.

"I think I left a drink at the bar, let's go back so I can finish it. I wouldn't want Will to throw it out." They laughed again and left the small cabin and strolled in the back door of the Casino.

Friday night. The crowd was thick by the time they returned to the bar. There wasn't a free chair or stool in the place, so Leslie and Tazia leaned against the end of the bar close to the kitchen. Leslie found her margarita and finished it off in one swift gulp. She held out the glass. "Pour me another one, Will. This is going to be a long night."

Before Tazia knew it, Leslie had left her alone again to schmooze with the customers. She was good at it. She meandered through the crowd, stopping to shake hands, introduce herself or hug an old friend, laugh and share a joke. On the surface, everything seemed right in the world. But Tazia knew that underneath her outer image, Leslie was a duck paddling like crazy to keep anyone from seeing the murky waters below.

It was a quarter to ten when Alfieri entered the bar and squeezed his way through the patrons to Tazia. He smiled with relief in his eyes when he got to her. "I'm glad you stayed inside and safe. Thank you." He turned to Will behind the bar. "Whiskey sour, please," he turned back to Tazia.

"Well, Leslie and I did go outside once, we had to walk around and through the alley to go to her cabin in back."

"I asked you…"

"No, you *told* me. And I don't deal well with being told. Just saying. At any rate, I had Leslie with me the whole time."

"Fair enough. You see anyone while you were out there?" Alfieri took his drink and sipped from the glass.

"We ran into Rex, that homeless guy that's been hanging around. I don't know what his deal is. But he took off when we startled him."

"Anything else?"

"No officer, that was it," Tazia said with a smirk on her lips and a sparkle in her eye.

"Fine. There's still no word from Claire the reporter. I just need you to…be safe. Okay?"

Tazia nodded and sipped a drink of her beer. "Okay." She winked at him then turned to watch the crowd.

"Excuse me folks," Brent the bushy bartender said to Tazia and Alfieri as he wedged his way past the end of the bar. "I need to get some more stock out. It's a busy night in here," he chuckled and wiped his hands on his apron. Disappearing into the crowd, Brent made his way across the room, unlocked the *Authorized Personnel Only* door and ducked into the storage area.

"What is it?" Alfieri looked down at Tazia who was squeezing his hand tight, her eyes as large as coasters. She gasped and held her breath for a moment. Fear prickled across her skin like a winter wind.

"I don't know, but it's like I can't catch my breath," Tazia wheezed as if she'd just been punched in the chest. She slid her beer onto the counter and grasped Alfieri's arm with both hands, looking up at him with pleading eyes. "She needs you."

The *Authorized Personnel Only* door slammed and Brent came running through the crowd knocking one lady down and not even stopping to help her back up. He ran past the bar and didn't stop until he was in the kitchen. He pressed a hand against his chest and held himself up holding his other hand against the door frame. Tazia and Alfieri rushed in behind him.

"What is it?" Alfieri asked.

"A girl, I…oh God…she's…" Brent turned to lean against the door frame and slid down to sit on the floor, he dropped his hands in his palms and shook his head. He was panting so hard he could barely talk, his face drained of color. "Call the police, paramedics, someone!" he cried in a panicked voice.

"Stay with him and call 9-1-1," Alfieri said, instinctively placing one hand over his gun neatly hidden under his jacket, and fought his way through the crowd to reach the other side of the room.

Tazia pulled out her cell phone and dialed emergency services. "Yes, this is Tazia Drake at the Casino Bar," she looked at Brent and touched his shoulder. He wiped his face with the back of his shirt sleeve. "Brent, what is it? What should I tell them?"

"Dead," Brent sucked in a shaky breath. "Dead girl… in the… old poker room." He dropped his face back into his palms and sat there, silent, shaking.

"Someone's dead, we need an ambulance and the police," Tazia said into the phone and stayed on the line until she heard the sirens blaring through the dark streets outside.

Making her way out of the kitchen, Tazia scanned the crowds for Leslie. Conversations were buzzing about Brent, but it didn't seem to taint the partying spirit of the customers. They didn't know what he had seen. She had to get to Leslie before the police got there. "There you are. Hurry, I need you," Tazia grabbed Leslie's arm and pulled her away from a conversation with two couples at one of the pool tables.

"Taz, I was in a…"

"Not anymore." When they got to the kitchen Brent was standing and drying the sweat from his face with a towel, Tazia looked at the bartender. "Do you know who she is?"

"No," Brent said on a heavy exhale shaking his head and squinting his eyes. "I just saw her…sprawled on the floor, her arms and legs twisted all…unnatural."

"What? What's going on?" Leslie looked at Brent then at Tazia. "Where's Chuck? I need Chuck. I can't do this. Something else bad's happened, hasn't it?" Her eyes filled with panic tears.

"We're not sure yet, but the police are on their way." The music from the sound system filled the room with Queen's song *Another One Bites The Dust*.

"What?" Leslie stuttered as she reached out to find something to hold her up. "What the hell?"

"Stay with Brent. I'll go find Alfieri," Tazia said patting her friend's shoulder. "Breathe."

Tazia filtered through the crowd buzzing with questions and trying to figure out what was going on. She reached the restricted access door and slowly opened it, then quickly closed it behind her.

"Stop right there," Alfieri stood in the center of the old poker room, opposite the storage pantry. "Don't touch anything! Don't even move or you'll mess up the footprints."

"Okay." Tazia stood like a statue, hands in her pockets, feet together, unwavering, perfectly still. "Is it Claire?"

"I don't know," Alfieri peeled off his rubber gloves, and watching his feet, backtracked out of the room using the same spots he'd entered on. "She's dead." He put his hands on Tazia's shoulders. "I know this is useless for me to say, but I'd feel much better if you'd let me take you home right now. And I don't mean to where you're staying here, I mean to Whisper Creek. This town isn't safe for you."

"Me?" Tazia looked into his eyes. His voice was so calm and sure but she knew he was holding something back. "Why me? Do you know who killed her?"

"No...of course not." But the look on his face told Tazia otherwise.

"But you know something," Tazia sighed looking past him and tilting her head at the young woman lying sprawled out on the floor behind him. "Who do you think she is?"

"I can't say."

"Can't? Or won't?" A shiver rocked Tazia's spine like a long cold wind. "The shadow man," she murmured.

"Say nothing about this. You understand?" Alfieri cautioned.

The sounds of the crowd on the other side of the door were muffled but present. The televisions, the room full of people drinking, talking and laughing. The click of pool balls hitting each other and the familiar Jimmy Buffett song playing on the sound system. And yet to Tazia, it all seemed a world away, an echo in the back of her mind.

Holding her steady, Matteo Alfieri cupped a hand under her chin and tugged her face up to look at him. "This is an active crime scene. You understand? You can't talk about it. You have to trust me." Tazia's eyes glistened with fearful tears and her heart pounded to the beat of the music.

What wasn't he telling her?

She felt as if the world had stopped moving. As if her lungs had stopped breathing and her heart stopped beating. Everything was suspended for a split second, although it felt like an eternity. She could see the dust motes hanging in the air, suspended motionless. Then all hell broke loose when the police and paramedics came crashing in. Tazia's knees buckled and Alfieri caught her.

CHAPTER FOURTEEN

Special Agent Matteo Alfieri sat at an empty desk in the Blaine County Sheriff's office in Hailey. They made minimal attempts to be accommodating, but clearly not happy to have an FBI agent poking his nose in their work. Matteo understood. It wasn't the first time he'd been in this spot.

Sheriff Rod Higgins was a tall strong man with black hair that was grey around his face. He motioned for Matteo to come into his office then turned to sprinkle flakes in the medium-sized fish tank behind his desk. The FBI Agent sat in a leather chair facing the Sheriff.

"Agent Alfieri, what can I do for you? Our recent events aren't a matter for the FBI." Higgins glanced at his computer screen then back at Matteo.

"The accidental death of the man in the attic of the bar is of no concern to me." Matteo leaned forward and narrowed his cold grey eyes on the sheriff. "But the murder of Claire Chandler, I suspect is part of an ongoing FBI case." Tazia was right to worry about Claire. The dead woman in the old poker room had been identified as the young reporter.

Sheriff Higgins stared at Matteo for a minute with a calculating look in his eyes. "I see. We don't want to impede an FBI investigation; however, until we're sure that's the case, this is a Blaine County Sheriff's investigation." His voice was stern, his eyes piercing. It was clear he didn't appreciate the feds invading his territory.

Matteo nodded appreciatively as he got up to leave the sheriff's office. He mulled over the facts as he poured himself a cup of coffee in the breakroom. Victor Nellis, mid-twenties, appeared to be an accidental death. Fell over a banister and down the stairs, died of a broken neck. Carl, the sheriff's computer geek, was working on breaking the passwords to Victor's phone and laptop to find some clues as to why the man was there and what he was doing. But again, that wasn't Matteo's main concern.

Claire Chandler was the real case. The twenty-three-year-old local, first year reporter at the Mountain Messenger wanted to make a name for herself at the paper. Had she caught the attention of the serial killer he'd been chasing? If it was the killer referred to as the Shadow Man, it opened up a whole different situation. The killer stalked female journalists, typically up to a week or more before striking. The FBI had been on the serial killer's trail for four years. Each year they got new clues, getting one step closer to identifying and apprehending him.

Taking the gold band off his little finger, Matteo twirled the memento of his late friend and partner, Niko. They had apparently gotten too close to the Shadow Man after his sixth victim, and Niko paid the price. It wasn't like this killer to go after men, but he'd no choice. Niko had gotten close enough to see his face. But he didn't live to tell about it.

Matteo realized he'd become obsessed with finding this killer. He had begun to lose touch with reality, thinking, breathing and living only to hunt down the Shadow Man. Then, as was the killer's M.O., he disappeared without a trace. He would lay low, and when attention appeared to be focused in other directions, he would strike again.

Now it looked as if he was here, in Ketchum, Idaho. Matteo had left the New York City office of the FBI and taken a liaison position with the Moon County Sheriff's Office because he had followed the scent of the serial killer to Idaho. But Matteo hadn't planned on falling in love with another journalist. That scared him more than anything. He was in a constant battle with himself over wanting to be with Tazia and wanting to not be with her in an effort to protect her. The Shadow Man's targets were all over the board. Young, old, big city, small town. The only thing that was always the same was that they were female journalists, bound and gagged, beaten and strangled. And always, a piece of newspaper, their newspaper, ripped and lying beside them. That's how he'd found Claire.

Victim one was Jill DeVall in Austin, Texas. Two was Brenda Malmber from Baton Rouge, Louisiana. Three was Brittany Stansell, a college student working on the campus newspaper in Miami, Florida. Four was Estella Torres in Atlanta, Georgia. It was clear he was on the move, and from what they could tell, never two in the same state. Victim five was Trina Kauffman in Columbia, South Carolina. Six was Darci O'Donnell in New York City, Matteo's home town. The killer laid low for nearly fourteen months before victim seven appeared in Omaha, Nebraska, Beverley Hodges. Matteo wouldn't have followed him across the country if it hadn't been for Niko. But he was on the case to stay now. Six months after Omaha, Jessica Cook, victim number eight was discovered in Denver Colorado, followed by number nine, Brooke Morrison, in Jackson Hole, Wyoming only six months later. The Shadow Man seemed to be stepping up his timetable since it was only three months after Wyoming that he killed a woman in Burley, Idaho. Maria Pew.

That's when Matteo decided to leave New York and take a post in Idaho. Clearly he needed more access to the Pacific Northwest, which was apparently where the serial killer was headed. If he could just cut him off, he could stop the trail of death by this madman. And Niko wouldn't have died in vain.

"Hey, Alfieri," Carl, the IT Specialist, said pulling up a chair to sit down at the side of the spare desk Matteo was camping out at. The Blaine County Sheriff's office wasn't large, but it did offer an empty desk for needs like this. "I have some news for you." Carl placed a cell phone and laptop on the desk. "There's no communication between Doug, the owner of these two items, and Victor, our dead guy. My guess is they never knew each other." He opened the laptop. "Most of the files on here are college papers and research."

The two looked at each other and Carl smiled big like he just won a hundred-dollar scratch ticket. "I'll bet Victor followed Doug, heard him mention the Casino here in town, killed the kid and headed here. He can't get the new owners to hire him, so he sneaks upstairs and starts digging for buried money. We saw the tools in his backpack, and there was evidence of him pulling boards and plaster away from the wall."

"But there wasn't any money there?"

"No. Doug's dad didn't hide any money or treasure in the building itself. Everyone here knows the old stories. He was simply referring to its real estate value. He used to own the entire block that the Casino sits on. A prime location in the heart of Ketchum, the most elite area in the state. This is where the affluent come to build their vacation homes. Movie stars, world leaders. But it's only real estate. Nothing more." Carl leaned back and snickered. "That's what he always meant by *money in the walls*."

"There was no evidence of anyone else up there with Victor? Someone who might have scared him? Caused him to fall over the banister and down the stairs? Someone to…push him?" Matteo asked.

Carl shook his head. "Nope. Not unless you believe the locals and the place is haunted. Maybe the ghost frightened him. But there were no prints of anyone else, and the staff and owner's alibi's all stand up. Even if someone did scare him, that's not foul play."

"No, it's not," Matteo agreed.

CHAPTER FIFTEEN

Saturday night, tee time, kick-off, whatever you were a fan of, the grand re-opening of the Casino Bar under new management was at lift off. Chuck had worked all afternoon with the help of the bartenders to rearrange the furniture to make room for a band to play in the back corner of the bar. Leslie had counted and re-counted the liquor inventory. Tazia was nearly dizzy swiveling back and forth on her bar stool watching the preparations. Every time she offered to help, someone would tell her to *stay out of the way, we've got this.*

"It's all under control," Tazia mumbled to herself as she watched them run back and forth like the circulation department trying to increase subscriptions. "Yep," she smirked taking a sip of her drink.

Local patrons and tourists were flowing in faster than shoppers on double-discount coupon day. Tazia relinquished her stool to new customers and stood out of the way as the crowd got so thick a hiccup could reverberate through the room like a recurring echo in the Grand Canyon. Tazia took another step backward, then another until she found herself in the doorway to the kitchen.

"Well isn't this cozy?" Tazia said to Tristan, the youngest of the bartenders. Tristan smiled and winked at her as he created appetizer trays on a production line. The empty trays were coming in faster than he could get the new ones back out.

"Yeah, and the crowds seem to be hungry, but at least they're not angry," Tristan laughed as he quickly filled three more trays.

"How much food are you guys giving away tonight?" Tazia asked.

"Leslie said only until this supply runs out, then the kitchen shuts down and I'll be out there at the bar with the other guys."

"The crowds might get angry then. Better don your armor!" They both laughed. Tazia edged her way to the end of the bar to watch the happy drinkers. The band was rocking. Reverend Horton Heat was a guest band after the local opening act. It was turning out to be quite a show. The energy level was high with people jumping up and down to the music. Tazia noticed while many of the people were bopping to the melody, they had earplugs in their ears. She figured that brought the volume down to an acceptable and enjoyable level. She rubbed her own ears and worried she may have a headache the next day from the combination of all the drinks and the extreme volume of the two bands.

Tazia turned to Will behind the bar. He was handing out drinks so fast he looked like a magician with his sleight of hand. "Hey, Will, how's the new drink doing? The Reveal?" Tazia had to shout even though she was standing right next to him. Will smiled, held a thumbs up signal, nodded in time with the tune, and kept the drinks coming. She laughed watching the bartenders all dancing behind the bar as they managed to serve drinks in time with the music.

A group of half a dozen men at the bar gave a loud cheer and raised their beers in an apparent toast pointing to a team's score on the muted overhead TV.

"Hey," Alfieri grabbed Tazia's arm. "I thought I asked you to go home."

"And I thought I explained why I couldn't," Tazia yelled back at him. She held up her drink, smiled and took a sip. "You should try The Reveal, it's awesome!"

"Fine, then I'm not leaving here," Alfieri barked as he scooted in beside her, crossed his bulging arms over his broad chest and watched the crowd.

"Suit yourself," Tazia snickered and took another swallow. She liked the new drink Leslie's bartenders had created. A tangy taste that tickled her tongue, and made her laugh.

"'Scuse me darlin'," Will the bartender said as he squeezed past Tazia heading for the kitchen. "I've got to get a breath of air before I pass out." He pushed his way through the kitchen and out the back door. The rush of cool air that came in with his exit felt good brushing across Tazia's cheek. The number of people in the bar drove the excitement level and the temperature up the scale. She picked up a napkin and wiped sweat off her forehead.

"Do you want a drink?" Tazia said into Alfieri's ear. He didn't speak, just shook his head 'no' and kept his eye on the crowd. She wondered what he was looking for? After finishing her third drink of the evening, Tazia stood in front of Alfieri, grinning and gyrating her hips. "Come on, dance with me," she yelled.

"Stay with me," Alfieri shouted back, not moving an inch.

"Fine, be that way," Tazia laughed as she bounced off into the crowd of jumping and dancing people. She got a glimpse of Alfieri every now and then as she weaved back and forth dancing with no one in particular. He stood steady, unmoving, not taking his eyes off of her.

Her bodyguard.

The band was near the end of their set when Tazia stopped dancing and leaned against Alfieri. It was that or slide to the floor and sit on his feet. The crowd hadn't diminished any, and the air was hot and stuffy.

There was no room to move. She glanced over at the bartenders and noticed that Will was still gone.

Tapping Alfieri on the shoulder, Tazia backed her way into the kitchen and found Leslie. "Hey, where's Will? Did he ever come back in?"

Leslie looked at the clock. "Good question, it's not like Will to skip out." She turned to look at Chuck who was cleaning up the kitchen, but he shrugged his shoulders not knowing either. Leslie poked her head around the corner to the bar area and waved Gorbs over. "Hey, how long's Will been gone?"

Gorbs shrugged with a glass in his hand getting ready to pour a beer. "I thought maybe he got sick or something. It's been a while, maybe two hours?" Gorbs excused himself and went back to work.

"Will's missing," Tazia told Alfieri. "He went out the back door a couple of hours ago for some fresh air and hasn't come back." Urgency and worry filled her voice.

"Hey Leslie," Dave shouted into the kitchen. "Where the heck is Will? He's disappeared and we need all hands mixing and pouring." Dave looked at her wide eyed then retreated back to his station behind the bar.

"You stay. I'll check it out," Alfieri said. He slid one hand inside his jacket hovering over his gun, then edged his way out the back door of the building. Tazia and Leslie exchanged worried looks.

Thirty minutes later the band was winding down for the night and the crowd had begun to dwindle. Tazia took up her post at the end of the bar but she still didn't see any sign of Will. She did notice Rex, the local homeless man sitting against the far wall with an empty plate in front of him. No doubt he snatched up everyone's leftovers from the free appetizers earlier in the evening.

The band began packing up their gear. Instruments taken apart and put in cases, cords coiled up and stowed away. Leslie turned the overhead jukebox music back on, but it wasn't nearly as loud as the band.

Clearly the two deaths earlier in the week hadn't deterred anyone from enjoying the grand re-opening night. It was a huge success.

Two bar stools opened and Tazia quickly slid onto one. "Ahhhh," she sighed. Her feet were starting to throb along with her temples. It had been a long night that by all accounts, started a week ago. Tazia smiled at Gorbs behind the bar. "How about a glass of ice water?" He smiled and slid a tall glass to her.

The four members of the band said their good-byes, waved at Leslie, Chuck and the bartenders, then chatted among themselves as they hauled their equipment out of the building. Leslie sat next to Tazia on a bar stool and let out a heavy breath.

Chuck and Dave got busy putting all the furniture back in place after the band's departure.

"I didn't think that many people were in town, much less would all be in here. I'm glad the fire marshal didn't stop by," Leslie said and ran her fingers through her curly hair.

"I think you pulled everyone in from the whole county!" Tazia chuckled, then her smile faded as she looked around more carefully. "Where's Alfieri?"

"And Will?" Leslie added. They looked at each other then back at the other bartenders. "Have you heard a word from Will? Have any of you tried to reach him?"

"Nothing," Brent said as he pulled his cell phone out of his pocket. He activated the screen and typed a quick text. "Not like Will to disappear with this kind of a crowd. Especially without saying anything to anyone."

"I'm worried," Leslie said looking across the room to her husband. "Chuck, have you heard from Will?"

Chuck glanced up at Leslie and shook his head.

"Well, Alfieri will find him," Tazia said reassuringly. At least, she hoped Alfieri would find the missing bartender, and that he'd be okay. "Maybe he sat down and fell asleep. Stranger things have happened."

"Will?" Leslie snorted. "Have you met that young man?"

"Yeah, I suppose you're right," Tazia sighed. "Still, I'm wagering nothing's wrong and there's a logical explanation." But her feelings didn't match her words.

"It better be a damn good explanation if he wants to keep his job!" Leslie huffed.

"Last call for alcohol!" Dave called out across the bar as he rang a bell to get everyone's attention. Several groups of people yipped and yelled and made their way to the bar.

"Anything? Any response?" Leslie asked Dave. He pulled his phone out to look at it and shook his head no.

"I've called his number five times in the last hour," Leslie said to Tazia.

Tazia gave her friend an understanding gaze and patted her on the back. "He'll turn up, you'll see."

After the last drink was served and the bartenders began their nightly end-of-shift duties, the front door opened. Dave closed out the till while Gorbs and Tristen gathered all the dirty dishes into trays for the dishwasher. Gorbs attacked all the tables and chairs with a wet towel cleaning every surface he could find. The front door opened and Alfieri strolled in shaking his head.

"I've looked everywhere within a three block radius. No sign of the guy. I assume there's no answer from him yet?"

"No response," Leslie said. "Trust me Agent Alfieri, this is not like Will."

"Now wait a minute," Gorbs walked up with a tub full of dirty dishes and the dish towel over his shoulder. "That's not entirely true. We've seen the kid duck out a couple of times in the past with no word, then show up the next day with a hangover."

"But not on a crucial night like this," Leslie protested. "Our grand opening? Will wouldn't leave us short-handed tonight."

Gorbs shrugged his shoulders as he hauled the dishes into the kitchen.

"I can alert your local police, but it's only been a few hours, so they won't do anything for a while." Alfieri looked at Tazia. "Any chance I can walk you home? Or, maybe you could walk me home?" Alfieri leaned in with a sultry sound to his voice and a sensuous tint to his grey eyes. "Stay with me tonight," he whispered into her ear.

"I thought you were staying in Hailey? I'm not walking to Hailey. And I'm not spending 'hiccup'... the night with you!" Tazia's words slurred from all the alcohol she'd drunk.

"It's not like that. The room has two queen beds. I'm not suggesting you sleep *with* me. I will just feel better if I know you're safe." Alfieri put a hand in the small of her back. "Although, if you wanted to…" he grinned.

Giving Tazia a wink, Leslie said, "Hey, all I ask is that you let me know if you stay someplace else tonight. I worry too much as it is." She dug in her purse for a moment and pulled out a pack of cigarettes. "Bound to be more comfortable than my couch."

Alfieri winked at Leslie and nudged Tazia toward the door.

"Where's your coat? Purse?" Alfieri asked.

"Um…" Tazia shrugged her shoulders. The long week caught up to her and she felt exhausted, barely able to stand. She slid down into a chair at an empty table and grinned with her eyes half-closed as Leslie handed Tazia's coat and purse to Alfieri. He leaned over the bar and said something to Dave, then came back and held up her coat so that she could slide into it. She wondered how many drinks she'd had and realized she lost count halfway through the second band set. Yep, she was going to have a doozy of a headache in the morning.

Maybe it was the alcohol, maybe it was the stress of the whole week that had finally come to an end, but Tazia collapsed without argument into Alfieri's car. She latched her seatbelt and closed her eyes. The next thing she knew Matteo Alfieri was holding her up and walking her into the back door of the Hailey Rest Stop hotel.

"Come on," Alfieri said. "You can have this bed, I'll sleep in the other one. Don't get in a state, I've got you." He helped her out of her clothes until she sat on the bed in nothing but her bra and panties. He slid her under the covers, kissed her forehead and turned the light out.

CHAPTER SIXTEEN

Matteo Alfieri sat in the corner of the room watching the beautiful sleeper in the next bed. He was already dressed and had a pot of coffee brewing on the counter. She twisted and moaned as the sun gently filtered its rays through the drapes. From the first time he saw Tazia, he knew this was a woman who would change his life. Somehow he knew she was the piece of the puzzle that would make him whole.

"I'm glad to see the Tazmanian Devil is alive," Alfieri said.

"Wamph," slipped out of Tazia's dry mouth. She rubbed her head and mumbled something else unintelligible as she rolled over to face him. She opened one eye, squinting at him and frowning. "Headache," she whispered.

"You mean, hangover," Alfieri got up and crossed the room. He came back and set a glass of water on the night stand beside her with a packet of aspirin. "I also have coffee ready after you take these." He sat down on the bed beside her and nodded to the chair in the corner of the room. "I laid your clothes out there. Get up and get dressed. I'm going to go down and get a newspaper and will be back in about twenty minutes." He couldn't help but smile at her. Even with a hangover and her long black hair matted and going in all directions, she was exquisite in his eyes. "You want me to pour you a cup of coffee before I leave?"

"Ummhmmph," Tazia mumbled and nodded yes. She closed her eyes again and buried her face in the pillow. "Wait," she angled her head around to look at him, her face still contorted with pain. "What do you mean... my clothes are over there? How did they..." Tazia fell back onto her pillow and held her eyes closed tight, pressing her palms against her temples.

"It's okay, I'm a professional, remember?" Alfieri laughed as he walked out of the room, closing the door behind him. He liked the idea that the hotel was small, security-wise, it reduced the risk of danger.

It was Sunday. The big event at Tazia's friend's bar was over. Maybe now he could convince her to go back home. For Alfieri though, there was still the matter of a murdered woman, a dead man, and a missing bartender as he picked up a paper and considered possible connections.

The Ketchum triple header, three cases at once.

He nodded at the lady behind the reservation desk and stepped out the front door for a moment.

The morning air was crisp and chilly as it rose off the river at the edge of the valley floor. The Wood River Valley was peaceful and beautiful. *Majestic*, he thought to himself as he viewed the morning mist that hung over the top of the mountains.

Doing the courteous thing, Matteo knocked on the hotel room door before he entered. He opened the door slowly. "You decent?" There was no answer, but he heard the shower running. He entered the room and smiled, noticing the clothes were gone from the chair. Sitting down by the window, he pulled the drapes open to let the sun in and unfolded the newspaper.

The shower stopped and Matteo glanced sideways in the direction of the bathroom. He wished they were in such a relationship that she would step out with nothing but a towel on in a blanket of steam. He grinned. *Perhaps someday.* He returned his attention to the newspaper and waited. The hairdryer whirred from the bathroom. He glanced at his watch and wondered if she was one of those women who spent hours getting ready. He hoped not.

The bathroom door opened slowly and a bank of moist air billowed out into the room. Tazia stepped out sluggishly, fully dressed – *darn*. "Breakfast?" Matteo asked hopefully.

"No," Tazia filled a coffee cup and sat down in the wooden chair at the small desk across from him. "The aspirin is starting to kick in. Thanks." She looked up at him as she blew the steam from the top of the coffee. "Any word on Will?" Her eyes still looked heavy, clearly affected by her hangover.

"Nothing yet. Leslie promised to let me know as soon as they heard something. If you want, I can drop you off at the bar, before I head over to the sheriff's office."

"What time is it?" Tazia asked and took a sip of her coffee.

"It's a quarter to twelve," Matteo looked at his watch then up into her soulful black Sioux eyes. "No hurry, whenever you're ready." He looked back down at the newspaper spread across his lap.

"I could use some food," Tazia mumbled with a slight grimace on her face.

"Let's go to that place in Ketchum, the one you like, then we can head to the Casino." He wanted to spend all day with her, but he had work to do. And the expression on her face told him she wasn't up for any adventures today. He figured with the look in her eyes, she'd probably be taking a nap in a few hours, and hopefully emerge early evening feeling better. Hangovers were a bitch that way, they just didn't like to let go.

"Perry's," Tazia whispered as she set the empty coffee on the desk beside her. "Maybe food will help." She stood up and looked around the room for her things. She scooped up her purse from the dresser and slid her arms into her coat that Matteo held out for her. He wanted to wrap his arms around her when she pulled it close, but he knew it wasn't appropriate. Not yet, anyway.

"So what did you think of the celebration last night?" Matteo asked as he opened the car door for Tazia. She looked up at him and winced. He walked around and got in the driver's seat and started the engine. "Or maybe," he continued. "I should ask if you remember the celebration last night?"

Pulling out of the parking lot and heading into Ketchum, Matteo noticed Tazia's eyes kept closing. "Would you rather just go to the Casino? They have that room upstairs next to the office with a bed in it. You could take a nap."

"No," Tazia said. "Food first, then nap." She let a small grin spread across her lips.

"Fair enough," Matteo said and turned the radio on just barely loud enough to hear. He knew any higher volume would probably hurt her head.

The deli café was about two thirds full as they entered the small building. Tazia asked for a chai latte and two poached eggs.

"I'll have your breakfast sandwich with ham," Matteo said opening his wallet to pay. He found them a booth away from the bright light of the windows, and Tazia scooted in, slumping over the table.

Setting the chai in front of Tazia, Matteo slid into the booth across from her. "Drink up, food will be here soon and in another twenty four hours or so, you'll feel human again." He chuckled as he watched her frown at him.

The waiter placed the two plates of food in front of Tazia and Matteo. Tazia seemed to hover over her plate taking in the warmth and smell of the food before reaching for utensils and eating. He smiled at her and took a bite of his breakfast sandwich.

Matteo remembered the last time he'd had a hangover this bad. It was two years ago, and one he would never forget. It was from a two-day binge after Niko, his best friend had died. He was hoping he'd never be sober again, never feel the pain of that loss. But on the third day he awoke with a throbbing in his head that was unparalleled in magnitude. All the rock bands in the world couldn't have been that loud. But awakening from that wasted state filled him with a new drive, and a realization of what he had to do. Niko's killer would be brought to justice.

He waited patiently for Tazia to finish eating. She nibbled at her eggs and sipped her drink. He wanted to talk to her about so many things, but clearly this was not the time. This was a time to be quiet, patient, and wait for her hangover to subside. He glanced at his watch.

"Is it time to go?" Tazia asked.

"I should get going soon. I have some things to follow up on and more questions about Will."

"I don't think I can eat all of this now," Tazia looked sadly at her plate. So far she had managed to nibble a third of one poached egg and drink most of her chai tea. "How about we get this in a to-go box and I can finish it later?"

"Of course," Matteo said. He got up to get her a Styrofoam box to put the rest of her meal in and a paper cup for the remainder of her chai. "Ready?" He held out a hand to help her up.

On Sundays the small mountain resort town was silent at mid-day with little traffic. Matteo walked Tazia into the Casino bar to make sure someone was there to greet her. He hated leaving her at all. It was a nagging feeling that she was in danger that tugged at the back of his mind. He wanted to keep her with him so that he could keep an eye on her, protect her. But he knew that was unrealistic thinking. They both had things to do. So for now, he let her go.

Matteo and Tazia had one very unusual gift in common, they both had a strong sixth sense. While he knew evil was lurking close by, he also felt pretty confident that she was safe inside the Casino today. As long and Leslie and the others stayed close by. And besides, he'd be checking in regularly.

"I'll stop back by later this afternoon. Maybe you'll feel better then?" Matteo kissed her forehead and left the bar.

Getting in his car, Matteo noticed Rex, the man who had been hanging around the Casino. He was sitting under a tree with an old sleeping bag behind him and his arms wrapped tightly around a large black plastic bag on his lap. Matteo considered whether the man wearing several layers of pants, sweaters jackets and even two hats might be interested in a hot cup of coffee. Instead of getting in his car, Matteo decided to walk around the corner to the Starbucks, buy two tall coffees, and bring one back for the homeless man.

"Hey man, you look like you could use a cup of joe." Matteo held out one cup to Rex. The man in many layers eyeballed the coffee with great enthusiasm as he reached for it, but shot an uneasy glance up at Matteo. "I'm Matteo. If you've got a minute, I'd like to ask you about something." The special agent knelt down on one knee to be less intimidating.

"You can ask, but don't know that I got anything to say," the old man muttered. "That's good stuff," Rex murmured, sipping the large coffee and easing back comfortably against the sleeping bag between him and the tree.

"You were seen last night behind the Casino bar. I was just wondering if you may have seen or heard anything unusual while you were out there?"

"This whole town's unusual in one way or another, don't ya' think?" Rex mumbled then took another drink.

"You have a point. But I'm looking for someone, a missing person who was also in that same area last night."

"Maybe…" Rex mumbled.

The two men sat in silence for a few minutes. Matteo knew he had to give people time to think, to answer when they were ready.

"Mmmm," Rex nodded his head as if remembering something. "Didn't see anyone, but I was in the alley pretty late. I remember hearing some kind of a scuffle then a large black SUV peeled out and skidded onto the main road."

"You're sure it was black?"

"Black, dark color. I know it wasn't white."

"Make or model?" Matteo asked.

"Big and expensive."

"Did you notice the license plate? Was it an Idaho plate, or from out of state?"

Rex took another sip of coffee and rolled his eyes before he let out a heavy sigh. "Did you get donuts too?" He smiled up at Matteo. "Didn't look at the plates. It was dark, I was half-asleep."

"Did you see anyone? How many people?" Matteo pushed for more details.

"Honestly, all I saw was the large dark SUV. Didn't see people. Just heard the scuffle."

"Did you see which way the vehicle went? Anything at all that could help me find it?"

"I heard voices. A man and a woman. They drove off through the alley and I went back to sleep. I didn't look to see where they were goin', none of my business."

"Thanks, pal," Matteo said as he stood up. He gave the man a ten dollar bill and got into his car.

Back at the county sheriff's office, Matteo prepared himself for the friction. It was just a known fact, local law enforcement agencies didn't always get along with the FBI, or anyone bearing three initials. But he did his best to ease the tension. He sat down with Sheriff Higgins and went over Will's disappearance and what Rex said. Matteo hoped his information was solid.

A scratchy voice came across the radio on the detective's desk. "Deputy Hackworth checking in. Just finished a citation, fifty-two in a thirty-five."

Higgins looked up at Matteo. "It's too soon to issue an alert, but we can keep our eyes open." Matteo nodded his approval. Higgins spoke into the radio on his desk. "Deputy Hackworth, we have a possible missing person in Ketchum. I want you to keep an eye on the house at 318 Fourth Street. Let me know if you see any movement." His tired eyes glanced back at the FBI Agent. "We good?"

"Sheriff, I'm only interested in the bartender's disappearance if it's a kidnapping.

Anything else is your jurisdiction. And as I said, as to the other cases, I only care about the murder of the journalist, which could be linked to an ongoing FBI investigation. I will be following up on that."

Higgins sat back in his leather chair with his chin cupped and resting in his hand. He stared at the computer screen for a minute, then squinted his eyes at Matteo. "If there's a serial killer in my county, I wanna to know about it."

"Higgins," Matteo said as he leaned forward, elbows on his knees, hands clasped under his chin. "You have my word if I find proof of our suspect here, you'll be the first to know. Right now, it's just a suspicion."

"Hell, it's always just a suspicion, even when we throw the handcuffs on them," Higgins smirked. "What's his M.O.? Are we looking at him striking again here?"

"No," Matteo shook his head and leaned back in the uncomfortable chair across from the sheriff. "Although if this is him, it's the first time he's killed more than one in the same state. I'd be very surprised if another body showed up. My goal is to track him down and stop him before he gets to his next location."

"What can you tell me?"

"Not much," Matteo said, rubbing the small gold ring on his pinky finger. "We don't have a name or even much of a description. Male, about six foot.

That's all we've ever been able to nail down for certain."

"Well damn, Agent Alfieri, that could be any one of a million."

"Exactly," Matteo sighed.

A voice crackled over the radio. "No sign of anyone here at residence in question, boss. I also did a walk around and everything looks secure."

"Thanks Hackworth," Sheriff Higgins replied. "Keep your eyes peeled for that SUV." He yawned and rubbed his puffy eyes before meeting Matteo's gaze. "What are the odds your buddy Will scored with some babe last night?"

"I'm sure that's possible, but I have a feeling it's not what happened."

"Any chance this is your serial killer?" Higgins asked.

"No. It's not his M.O. I think we've got three unique cases, each with their own motives, and perpetrators. The Ketchum triple header," Matteo said the last little bit under his breath.

"Sheriff," Hackworth's scratchy voice came over the radio again.

"Yeah, go ahead," Higgins replied.

"I've got a dark SUV that just pulled away from the bar heading southeast out of town and I'm keeping it in sight."

"Affirmative." Higgins turned back to Matteo.

"Does Pritcher, the developer, own any properties around here?" Matteo had a hunch. Higgins opened his computer screen and scrolled through some pages.

"Here we go," Higgins copied the address of two places onto a note pad and handed it to Matteo.

"Are either of these southeast out of town?"

"Both of them are," Higgins said with an understanding look in his eye.

Matteo nodded his thanks and got up from the chair. "I'll check back in with you later."

"Appreciated," Higgins said as he pulled a file folder from the corner of his desk and opened it.

Pulling out his cell phone as he strolled back out to his car, Matteo texted Tazia.

MATTEO: *You still okay?*

He waited for an answer.

TAZIA: *Still okay*, followed by an emoji with the eyes scrunched closed and the tongue sticking out.

It made Matteo chuckle. Still hungover is what she was really saying. He plugged in the first address on his phone to get directions. It wasn't far, about five miles out of town.

The black SUV was nowhere in sight as Matteo drove out of one resort town and through the beautiful expanse of wealthy ranches and mansions that dotted the regal mountains. He followed the arrows on his phone's GPS and turned onto a side road leading to the river and a forested hillside. The road switched from pavement to gravel as it neared the river and an older looking ranch. The house was smaller and appeared to be empty. He slowed to about fifteen miles an hour and surveilled the property as his car crunched down the gravel road. A large fenced pasture that probably once held horses was now empty. A fairly nice barn stood on the far end.

No dark SUV here. Matteo drove to the edge of the road a few yards from the barn to find a place to turn around when he noticed the nose of a beige sedan poking out from behind the building. He'd seen that car before in front of the Casino. He eased his foot up letting the car creep even slower as he focused on the details of the sedan. Blaine County license plate. He picked up his note pad and jotted down the make and model along with the plate number. Then he saw it. The real estate sticker in the window and the name in large letters – DONNA SANCHEZ. The pieces were starting to fall into place. He pulled off the gravel and parked his car in a small grove of trees. She could be showing the property to a prospective buyer, although he didn't see any For Sale signs. Maybe she lived here, or maybe, just maybe, she was up to no good. Matteo stepped cautiously across the loose rock and dirt as he approached the back of the barn.

A man and a woman were arguing inside the barn. "This has gotten way out of hand. I'm done here," the woman's voice scolded.

"What do we tell Titus?" a man's voice growled.

"Titus can take a flying leap as far as I'm concerned. I'm not getting into any more trouble for that guy."

"But what about the bartender?"

"No sale is worth this much hassle," the woman screeched.

Matteo looked into the barn, but didn't see Will anywhere. He heard a noise out in the field and glanced up to see Will running through the large pasture toward the road. Matteo took a step back and pulled the cell phone out of his inside pocket. He had saved Sheriff Higgins's number and tapped the call button. He whispered into the phone as he strolled back to his car. "Higgins, this is Alfieri. I'm at the old ranch house location you gave me for Titus. Will was being held here by Donna Sanchez and some thug. But it looks like Will got away on his own and is heading back home. I'll see if I can pick him up and give him a ride." He ended the call and slid the phone back in his pocket.

The red headed woman dressed in a tight fitting dress and boots that came up over her knees stomped across the dirt floor, stormed out of the old barn and gasped when she swerved and saw Agent Alfieri getting into his car.

"Son of a…I swear," Donna sputtered as she shook her head and leaned back against the door of her car. "This day just keeps getting better!"

"All this for a lousy piece of real estate," the man huffed angrily at Donna as he stomped out of the barn.

"Shut up, moron," she barked.

"I wouldn't leave town if I were you," Matteo warned, then shut his car door and took off down the lane heading back to the highway. He pulled off the side of the road just ahead of Will and waved for the tired-looking young man to join him. Will stopped, looked back at the barn in the distance, and jogged across the road to get into Matteo's car.

The young bartender wiped his mouth with the back of his sleeve. "Man, I really need a cup of coffee."

"I'll take you into the station, you'll have to give them your report. They'll have coffee there," Matteo said.

"What do I need to report?" Will asked.

"Just tell them what happened. They'll ask if you want to press charges." He looked at the dirty rumpled bartender. "That's up to you. Are you hurt?"

"No," Will winced letting his head drop against the headrest. "Just tired and hungry. And in need of caffeine."

CHAPTER SEVENTEEN

Leslie and Tazia sat facing each other in the upstairs office of the Casino. Leslie pulled a cigarette out of its pack and flicked the lighter to the end of it. She leaned back into the soft couch as she inhaled. "What now? What happens now?" Leslie asked.

"Will didn't file charges against Donna and her henchman, so they go free. As for Titus, there's no evidence he actually did anything illegal. Forensic gathering is done in the attic and you can access it now. I noticed they still have the first floor room taped off."

"Well, Will asked for a week's vacation, and I don't blame him," Leslie chuckled and let the cigarette smoke drift out of her mouth.

"Do me a favor," Tazia said as she stuffed her laptop into its case and rounded up the last of her things from the second-floor office. "Don't buy any more businesses, at least for a long time." She smiled at her friend on the couch.

"You can count on it. Are you heading home today or tomorrow?"

"First thing tomorrow morning. Gotta' get back to work and make sure I still have a job." She laughed. Leslie stood up and gave her a hug.

"I've got some errands to run, but catch you later for a drink?" Leslie put her cigarette out in the ashtray on the edge of the desk and winked at Tazia before leaving the room.

Tazia picked up her tote bag and laptop, and glanced down the hall toward the dark entrance to the third floor. There was no treasure up there. In the end, it was nothing more than lumber and plaster, and old memories.

Walking downstairs, Tazia stopped for a moment and peered at the door of the large storage room where Claire's body had been found. The memory of the crime weighed heavy on her nerves. She could barely make out the supernatural echoes left behind by sadness and violent death. She shuddered.

Sunday evening Tazia and Leslie sat at the bar mulling over the week's events. Victor was a wanted man, now dead. The only thing they could figure was that something startled him, causing him to fall over the railing and to his death on the stairs below.

The only mystery left was the murder of Claire. Alfieri was holding something back, Tazia was sure of that. But he wouldn't say what.

"Here's to the most successful grand re-opening ever," Tazia held her glass up to Leslie's for a toast.

"I couldn't have done it without you," Leslie said. They both took a drink and chuckled. There were a handful of patrons in the bar on Sunday night. Locals. Playing pool, watching an NFL football game on TV, having drinks, chatting and laughing.

"I'll have a Guinness," Alfieri said as he strolled into the bar and slid onto the stool beside Tazia. "Are you going home tomorrow?"

"Are you?" she asked him.

"I still have a few things here to check out on the murder case, but I'll be heading down tomorrow or Tuesday." Alfieri picked up his dark beer and took a healthy swig. "I like your place," he said to Leslie. She smiled and nodded her thanks.

"Any chance I can take you out to dinner," Alfieri asked Tazia as he leaned in, his mouth so close to her ear it made her shiver.

"I…" she looked at Leslie.

"Go ahead. Chuck and I have plans for tonight. Now that all this is over, I'm going to collapse in the cabin with him and a gallon of whiskey. These guys can take it from here, at least for the next few days," Leslie said looking over at Dave behind the bar.

"Dinner?" Alfieri asked again, his fingers fidgeting on the edge of his beer glass.

"What did you have in mind?" she looked into his winter grey eyes and saw promise there. It made her smile sheepishly.

"You, me, some quiet dimly lit place." Alfieri's smile made her stomach do a triple summersault. He finished his beer then helped Tazia with her coat. They walked outside of the bar where they stopped, and leaned against the fence.

"Maybe an after dinner drink in my hotel room." Alfieri bent down, took her mouth and lightly kissed her lips, then more deeply. All the needs Tazia had held inside for so long broke free in a crazed stampede that trampled all thought of restraint or caution, and she kissed him back. Fully. Completely. Her heart accelerated, her pulse quickened and her whole body ached for more.

"Meow," a black cat above them called out. Tazia glanced up at the cat sitting in the third floor window of the Casino.

"That Leslie's cat?" Alfieri asked.

"No, Leslie doesn't have a cat." They looked back up at the window and the cat was gone and in its place was a woman offering an approving smile as she slowly retreated from the light into the shadows of the attic and faded away like smoke from an extinguished candle.

Alfieri touched Tazia's shoulder then slowly ran his hand down her arm to her hand. Even through the sleeve of her jacket the touch sent little sparks exploding through her body. Her eyes burned with tears of want, need, and desire. Longing that she'd held in far too long was finally released and she gave in to it. Tazia wove her fingers through his and gripped his hand. Her eyes told him what she could not.

THE END

ABOUT THE AUTHOR

Be sure to post a review to help other readers find this book. It's greatly appreciated!

Be sure to sign up for my newsletter so you'll be the first to get notices of new book releases.
www.sherrybriscoe.com

Sherry Briscoe is an award-winning author of mystery, suspense, and supernatural thrillers. Her childhood heroes were Alfred Hitchcock and Edgar Allan Poe, and she insists that episodes of *The Twilight Zone* made perfectly fine bedtime stories. A native Idahoan with Cherokee heritage, she holds degrees in Journalism, Photography, and Adult Education. She is a world traveler, US Army Veteran, founder of the Idaho Screenwriters Association, active board member of the Idaho Writers Guild, Romance Writers of America, Women's Fiction Writers Association and professional speaker and workshop facilitator.

You can also follow me on Bookbub where you can get free and discounted books.

I'm on Facebook too!

Other books by this author include:

Fine Line of Denial

Mists of Garibaldi: *Tales of the Supernatural*

The Man In Number 7

Forgotten Lives

Shattered Souls

www.sherrybriscoe.com